The Calico Heart

by

Patricia Kiyono
and Stephanie Michels

The Calico Heart
by Patricia Kiyono and Stephanie Michels
Published by Astraea Press
www.astraeapress.com

This is a work of fiction. Names, places, characters, and events are fictitious in every regard. Any similarities to actual events and persons, living or dead, are purely coincidental. Any trademarks, service marks, product names, or named features are assumed to be the property of their respective owners, and are used only for reference. There is no implied endorsement if any of these terms are used. Except for review purposes, the reproduction of this book in whole or part, electronically or mechanically, constitutes a copyright violation.

THE CALICO HEART
Copyright © 2013
PATRICIA KIYONO, STEPHANIE MICHELS
ISBN 13: 978-1482319569
ISBN 148231956X
Cover Art Designed by For the Muse Designs

From Patricia Kiyono: For my fellow quilters at the Helping Hands Quilt Guild of Fairhaven Ministries. Your fellowship and support have sustained me through many difficult times, and I have been blessed to work with you.

From Stephanie Michels: For Mom, who always believed in me, this one is for you.

To Melanie Ranta,
When you have to go to the doctor's office, it's a comfort to have Melanie there. Thanks for always being so patient and willing to talk. Hope you enjoy this. Happy reading!
Stephanie Michels
7-24-2014

Chapter One

"Bye, Mom! Bye, Dad! Love you!"

"Bye, honey. Love you, too," Sylvia Miller called back then laughed as a shower of iridescent bubbles surrounded her daughter Lynne and new son-in-law.

The tiny orbs floated around the couple, blending with the sparkling beadwork on Lynne's sweeping wedding gown and adding gemlike twinkles to her veil. The newlyweds laughed with delight as they raced, hand-in-hand, through the bubbles blown at them by the wedding guests. Her daughter looked like Cinderella rushing down the castle steps to her carriage. Only this time, it was a gaily decorated, red Mustang convertible, and her handsome prince was right at her side.

Wasn't it just yesterday that Lynne and her older brothers had been playing make-believe in the big sandbox in the backyard?

The time had flown by so quickly. The kids' mud pies and toy cars had quickly given way to rock posters and laptop computers when they'd reached their teens. Now, her babies had grown up and left the nest. The boys both had thriving careers in Chicago, and Lynne was moving on to a new life with Ron.

As always, Dave seemed to read her mood. His arm tightened around her waist. She leaned into him, grateful for his unspoken comfort, as she continued to wave to the newlyweds until their convertible disappeared from sight. Their guests returned to the air-conditioned comfort of the church hall, but Sylvia remained outside with her family, blinking back the nostalgic tears that clouded her vision. It wouldn't do to be caught crying on such a joyous occasion.

Too late.

"Waterworks alert." Dave Junior's cheeky warning told Sylvia she'd been busted. "Mom's about to cry," he added with a grin.

Her eldest son resembled his father more every day. They were both tall and handsome in their tuxes. However, D2—as the family called him—appeared to be a lot more comfortable in formalwear than Dave was. Her poor hubby had fidgeted with his starched collar ever since he'd put it on that morning. He'd done the same thing on their own wedding day.

More tears blurred her vision at the tender memory. She blinked again then lifted her chin and returned her son's smile. "I am not!"

"You really expect us to believe that?" Her middle child chuckled. John was a couple inches shorter than his father and brother but shared their good looks. Now, his brown eyes twinkled as he leaned down to touch his forehead against hers. "Admit it, Mom, you've cried at every major occasion in our lives."

"Major?" Dave echoed. "Are you kidding? Boys, your mother would cry at a stop sign if it reminded her of one of you."

"Can I help it if I'm so proud of my family?"

Her husband sent their sons a knowing look. "All I can say is it's a good thing I have a decent job. I could retire in luxury on the small fortune I've spent on her waterproof mascara all these years."

"Oh stop it," she protested and gave him a playful swat on the arm. "I'm not that bad,"

Her husband chuckled and gave her the killer smile that had won her heart back when he was a varsity football player and she was a lowly high school sophomore. Time might have threaded gray through his wavy, black hair and thickened his waistline a bit, but even after twenty-six years of marriage, that smile could still make her go weak in the knees.

Twenty-six years. It was hard to believe so much time had passed since the day they'd been the young couple driving away on their honeymoon. Of course, she and Dave had only headed from their quiet ceremony to the cozy home they'd purchased—the same ranch home in the suburb of Grandville, Michigan, where they had raised their family and still lived. Lynne and Ron, on the other hand, were heading to the airport for a romantic two-week getaway in Europe.

Sylvia envied them a little. She'd always wanted to travel but had never been further from Grand Rapids than a few camping weekends on the shore of nearby Lake Michigan. Still, she had no regrets. She and Dave would have the time to travel once they both took their early retirements. She'd already resigned her position as a professor of mathematics at Grand Valley State University. The board had accepted her letter of notice at the end of the semester. Soon, Dave would retire from his CPA position with Davis Andrews, a prestigious national consulting firm. She smiled, thinking of the thick bundle of travel brochures she'd stashed in the drawer of her sewing table just waiting for that day to finally arrive.

"...should have let one of the boys drive them to the airport," Dave grumbled now as he held open the foyer door for her. The boys had apparently gone inside while she'd been lost in her thoughts.

Probably to avoid the usual lecture on thriftiness, she thought, turning her head to hide her amusement.

"Long-term parking is such a waste of money," Dave continued. "They've already spent far more than they should have on this honeymoon. Ron and Lynne could have made a substantial down payment on a house with all that they're blowing on the next two weeks."

"Honey, Ron already has a beautiful home in Heritage Hills. Lynne loves it."

"Maybe so, but those old homes need a lot of upkeep. Do you have any idea how much it costs nowadays to replace a boiler or a heat pump in one of those places?"

Sylvia smiled indulgently as they took the steps down to the church's family center in the lower level. *Leave it to my conservative CPA to think of furnaces on a glorious June evening.*

"And what if Lynne gets pregnant?" he asked. "Or Ron could lose his job. Anything can happen in this economy. They should have put the money in the bank so they'd be prepared."

Sylvia smiled and hugged him affectionately. "Oh, David Miller, I love you!" she declared.

He stopped on the landing while she was still on the step above him and turned. Leaning forward, he brushed his lips against hers and murmured: "Even after all these years?"

"Hmm, let me think about that." She pretended to consider the idea.

"Maybe this will help," he suggested, wrapping his arms around her. He pulled her toward him then lowered his lips to deliver a kiss so passionate it nearly took her breath away. He pulled her closer, molding her body against his and kissed her again.

"Oh, yeah," she whispered when they broke from the intimate embrace. "Even after all these years."

"Well that's good," he replied. He brushed his fingers over her cheek. "Because I love you, too, Sylvie, more every day."

He gave her a quick kiss then held out his arm to her. "Shall we rejoin our guests?"

She nodded happily. With his arm around her waist, they went down the remaining steps to the family center.

The church's wedding coordinator had done a wonderful job with simple decorations. With Dave and the boys' help, she'd draped the ceiling with huge swags of white chiffon fabric. Inside the folds, she'd tucked dozens of sapphire blue and pale teal balloons to match the colors of the bridesmaids' dresses. Suspended in the center of the ceiling, where the swags met, was a huge pair of white wedding bells surrounded by spirals of ribbon in the same sapphire and teal. In the middle of each of the hall's tables, blue and teal gerbera daisies floated in a glass bowl centerpiece. Now that the festivities had wound down, Sylvia could take a moment and savor the lovely setting. She and Dave moved around the room, visiting with their guests, chatting leisurely, and making certain everyone had had enough to eat and drink.

"I see Sue and Ellen already have things almost packed up," Sylvia remarked as they neared the long, linen-covered table where two of her best friends, Ellen Wheeler and Sue Visser, had presided over the display of wedding gifts. Now, the two women were busily boxing up the gifts and cards to make it easier to transport them home.

"Want me to find the boys so they can carry some of this stuff to our car before they head back to Chicago?" Dave asked.

She nodded. "Great idea. I'll help the girls pack up whatever is left. It shouldn't take us more than a few minutes to finish."

He gave her a quick hug then went to find their sons. Sylvia's friends looked up as she joined them then hurried over to give her big hugs.

"Everything went so well, Syl!" Ellen exclaimed. "Lynne made such a beautiful bride."

"You look lovely, too." Sue agreed, continuing to tape shut the box she held. "You always look lovely, but that shade of blue is stunning with your black hair."

"Thanks. It's Dave's favorite color," Sylvia told them then motioned to the pile of boxes on the table. "What can I do to help?"

"Just stand there and talk to us. We're almost done," Ellen replied, reaching for the next gift. It was the exquisite bedspread their quilting group had finished for Lynne and Ron. The newlyweds had opened it before dinner so everyone could admire it.

"Let me have that one," Sylvia said and reached out to take the beautiful gift. She ran her hand over it, lightly tracing the dainty stitches with a fingertip. "I still can't believe we got it done in time."

"We probably wouldn't have if it hadn't been for Lila," Ellen said then looked behind Sylvia and laughed. "Speak of the old slave driver, and here she is."

"Did I just hear you call me an 'old slave driver,' Ellen Wheeler?" a petite older woman with carefully tinted blonde hair bustled up to them.

"How about if I just say 'here's our slave driver now'?"

"That's much better." Lila Haggerty nodded. She might have celebrated her seventy-fifth birthday recently, but the little dynamo would be the last person to acknowledge her age. Besides, she could still run circles around most of them. She gave Sylvia a quick hug then paused to admire the quilt. "This is definitely one of the prettiest quilts I've had the pleasure of working on."

"I could never have done it without you," Sylvia said. "All of you. I can't find words to thank you enough."

"No thanks are needed," Sue and Ellen said almost as one voice.

"You would have done the same if it had been one of us," Lila added. "Everyone knows that. Besides most of us have watched Lynne grow up. So this is our way of showing her our love."

The Wedding Ring quilt had been a gift of love from start to finish. Sylvia had special ordered the fabric for it, laid out the pattern under Lila's watchful eye, then had painstakingly hand-stitched the design pieces herself. Afterwards, Sue, Ellen, and the other women in the quilt group had come forward to help assemble the blocks and hand-quilt the patterned top to the batting and plain backing. Lila had been even more determined than Sylvia to finish this quilt in time for the wedding. She'd organized the other quilters and went to the Stitching Post herself every day in order to oversee the time-consuming hand quilting. The other women had worked under her direction so every stitch was uniform and perfect. The spritely widow had far more quilting experience than anyone else in the group. In fact, over her lifetime, Lila had probably made more quilts than all of them combined, and each quilt was a masterpiece of exquisite handwork, so the others were happy to learn from her.

Sylvia felt blessed to have such caring and loving friends. Their friendship went back a long time, almost to the days when she'd been a newlywed. In those days, she and Dave hadn't had much money, so they'd always been on the lookout for inexpensive entertainment. One weekend, they had visited a local quilt show and stopped to admire the beautiful pieces on display in Lila's booth. Sylvia told the quilter how she'd always wanted to try her hand at the craft. That's when Lila invited her to a small quilt shop in Grandville, The Stitching Post, where she and a few other women met each week to sew and socialize.

"We're a modern day quilting bee, but thankfully minus the corsets and petticoats," Lila had told her with her impish grin. "You should visit the group."

Intrigued, Sylvia checked out the store the following Monday. While she was there, she met Myra Hodges, the store's friendly owner, as well as Sue and Ellen who had happened to be shopping that afternoon. They'd also invited Sylvia to come back on Tuesday evening to meet the others. The next evening, Sylvia had kissed Dave goodbye after dinner and returned to The Stitching Post. She'd met the rest of the group and learned they were making lap quilts to donate to the veteran's home for Christmas. The women had told her to pull up a chair then shared some of their own fabric scraps so she could lend a hand. With Lila's help, Sylvia had started on her very first quilt that night Over the years, as the hobby gained popularity, the small group grew from the handful of friends to a congenial group of more than two dozen members. Housewives and professional women, newlyweds and retirees. The friends ranged in age from early twenties to a new member who'd decided to take up quilting for her eightieth birthday.

"We're as different as the various fabrics in this quilt," Sylvia mused as she tucked the precious gift under her arm and carried it outside to the car.

Chapter Two

"It was such a beautiful wedding," Sylvia remarked as she sat at the bedroom vanity to tissue off her make-up later that evening. "The weather was perfect. Not too hot, not too cold. This late in June, you never know what you'll get."

"I'm just glad to finally get out of this blasted tuxedo," Dave replied, tugging loose his tie and starting on the button of his heavily starched shirt.

"You looked very handsome." She met his eyes in the mirror and winked suggestively. "Sexy."

"I felt like a stuffed penguin. I don't know why we had to have all the fuss."

"Honey, she's our only daughter. We had to do things up right for her wedding."

"She'd have been just as married with a simple ceremony and reception in our rose garden. Just think what we could have saved on the flowers alone."

"We would never have been able to fit all of our friends and co-workers—and Lynne and Ron's—in our backyard," Sylvia said, repeating the same argument she'd given him when he'd first suggested a home wedding. "The church hall was the perfect solution. And we didn't have to worry about rain or having a guest fall in the pool. Besides, it's not like we didn't have money already saved." She grinned. "I think you rushed to the bank straight from the hospital the day Lynne was born so you could set up a savings account for her wedding."

"Nah. I waited until the next day," he admitted, sheepishly. "But we still went over budget..."

"A little," Sylvia conceded, remembering a few bills she still hadn't slipped into the pile of expenses on his desk. "But certainly nothing that will jeopardize our retirement plans."

Dave mumbled something, but with his head buried in their closet, she couldn't hear his exact words.

"Look under your side of the bed," she called.

"What?"

"Your slippers. That's what you're looking for, isn't it?" She slathered a bit of extra moisturizer on her forehead where she'd noticed a few deep lines had recently appeared. "I think you left them under your side of the bed."

Her husband crossed to the bed, bent to look under it, then held up the missing slippers with a triumphant smile. "Found 'em!"

"Whatever would you do without me?" Sylvia deadpanned.

He pursed his lips and pretended to consider the idea. "Go barefooted?"

"You hate going barefoot. I guess you'd better keep me around."

"Oh, I don't know," he said, coming to stand behind her chair. He leaned down and wrapped his arms around her then rested his chin on the top of her head. Meeting her eyes in the mirror, he smiled. "Just think how much I could save on your mascara alone."

She laughed and swatted his arm. "As if you'd even know how much mascara costs. That's one of the things my paycheck always covered."

"Are you going to miss it?"

"The paycheck?"

"Well, that and the students. I know how much you love teaching."

"I did love it. It was great being able to help kids understand math. The looks on their faces when they suddenly got it—when they went from struggling to understanding—" She paused and smiled. "It was priceless."

"Was it like that when you tutored me?"

She nodded. "Always. I love helping kids get to that *ah-ha* moment. But, now, I'm ready to move on to other, more exciting, experiences."

"What do you mean?" He straightened and headed back to the closet to hang up his tux jacket.

"Our travel plans, honey." She rested her elbows on the vanity and cupped her chin in her hands, letting her imagination roam. "Oh, Dave, there are so many places I've been dying to see. I can hardly wait until you retire, too, so we can take off.

"Where would you like to go first? I've always wanted to visit the Texas Quilt Museum, but that's pretty far for our first trip. I thought maybe we could head up north, to see the Mackinac Bridge and visit Mackinac Island. Tahquamenon Falls, too. Did you know the locals call them Root Beer Falls because of their–"

"That may have to wait a bit," Dave interrupted her spiel. "We have all these extra wedding expenses now. We need to take care of them. We agreed we wouldn't tap into our retirement savings to pay for any of them, right?"

"Of course," she agreed. "But there aren't that many bills left to pay. Besides, it doesn't cost anything to dream."

He shrugged then reached in his dresser drawer for a pair of pajamas. "I think I'll grab a quick shower."

****

Dave lingered in the bathroom, postponing the time before he had to face Sylvia again. He'd seen the determined look in her eyes when she started talking about retirement and travel plans. He suspected she wouldn't let the subject drop and would continue their discussion. He didn't want to argue, but he wished he could make her understand that traveling was too expensive. Davis Andrews provided generous pension benefits for their employees, but the payout was severely reduced if you retired early. Sylvia had also made good money as a math professor, but early retirement had decreased her pension, too. Still, they'd be able to live comfortably enough until they were old enough to collect their Social Security benefits—*if* they lived frugally and stayed within their means. For the next few years, they'd need to watch their hard-earned savings and carefully plan any necessary expenditures. *Necessary* certainly didn't include throwing money away for something as frivolous as travel.

He refused to be like his parents. They had been a perfect example of what happened when people didn't pay attention to their finances until it was too late. He'd been young when they died, but his grandfather had told him how they had lived like there was no tomorrow. They'd bought new cars and airplanes—who on earth owned their own airplane?—thrown big parties and taken expensive vacations. When they died in a plane crash—in a plane his father had been piloting—there'd barely been enough money to bury them.

Their death had shaken up his life. His sister, Muriel, had been in college; his brother, Bill, was a senior in high school; but Dave had only started fifth grade. His parents had left them with the housekeeper while they flew to Los Angeles for a few days for a conference. Dave had been surprised when his grandfather had come to his school in the middle of the day to pick him up, but he'd been too young to be alarmed.

He'd started to worry, however, when they got home and found Muriel and Bill waiting there. His grandfather had marched them into the living room and delivered the news in a stern, disapproving voice: their parents were dead.

Dave and his siblings had been given until the following day to pack the things they wanted, then they'd moved into his grandfather's house. His parents' house had been sold to pay off bills. As young as Dave had been, he'd still understood enough of what had happened to feel humiliated about having to depend on others' charity. He'd vowed he would never let anything similar happen when he had a family of his own.

Meeting Sylvia had changed Dave's life again. His grades had seriously tanked his senior year, so his football coach had enlisted Syl's help as a tutor. Although she was only a sophomore, Sylvia was the top student in her math class and had a determination to succeed. She was also the most beautiful girl Dave had ever seen. The minute she'd smiled at him, he'd fallen for her. He'd hardly been able to concentrate during their first tutoring session, instead he'd tried to get up the nerve to ask her to go out with him. Unfortunately, she'd rushed off before he could. The next day, when he'd tried to talk to her after their session, she'd said she had to hurry home. After a few more excuses, he'd figured she didn't want to date a loser like him. That was when he'd buckled down and had managed to bring up all of his grades, not just the one in math. Unfortunately, the only thing the improved grades had done was end his need for tutoring sessions with the cute little brunette.

However, thanks to her, Dave had discovered an aptitude for numbers and had gone on to study accounting at Grand Valley State. It had been his lucky day, when he'd run into Sylvia there three years later in the college bookstore. Dave had decided it was a second chance for him, and he wasn't about to blow it. He'd hurried over to say hello then had asked her out for coffee before he lost his nerve, and was floored when she'd accepted.

They made an unlikely pair. Syl loved to laugh and be around people. Whenever they attended parties, he could always find his outgoing wife in the thick of things. People gravitated to her, enjoying her company. He, on the other hand, was more introverted. He preferred quiet evenings at home. Surprisingly, they complemented each other like salt and pepper. They seldom argued and liked most of the same books and music and had similar priorities. They'd both had good careers, raised three great kids, and built a comfortable life together.

So why did Sylvia suddenly want to change all that? Retirement. Travel. Spending money frivolously.

Why couldn't his wife be content with things just as they were?

Chapter Three

"Sorry I'm late," Sylvia apologized as she rushed into The Stitching Post the following Tuesday evening for the weekly group meeting.

"Don't worry." Myra gave her a reassuring smile. "You've got plenty of time, honey. A new delivery of holiday fabrics came in yesterday, so most of the gals are busy browsing through them. You know how it is with us quilters. We always need more fabric."

Sylvia grimaced. "I know. Dave says I have enough material in my sewing room to start a shop of my own."

"What do you think?" Lila asked, entering the shop in time to hear the exchange.

Sylvia grinned mischievously at her spritely friend. As always, Lila was meticulously dressed and coiffed. Tonight, she wore a plum-colored pantsuit that complimented her coloring beautifully. "I think we should check out Myra's new shipment."

"Couldn't have said it better myself," the older woman agreed. She held up her own bulging scrap bag. "There's always room for a few new squares. What do you say we stow our stuff first then go take a look at the new fabric?"

The two women made their way to the back corner of the shop, where a couple dozen chairs had been arranged in a cozy grouping. They greeted some of the other quilters, who were already seated and setting up their projects for the evening. Lila tossed her bag on the seat of an upholstered armchair. Everyone knew Lila preferred to sit there, so they always kept it open for her. Sylvia put her own bag on the seat of the straight-backed, wooden rocker to Lila's left.

"What are we going to work on now that Lynne's Wedding Ring quilt is finished?" Lila asked as they joined their friends by the display of new fabric.

"How about a Christmas table runner?" Sue suggested. The plump brunette held up length of white fabric sprigged with embroidered holly. "Wouldn't this be pretty with a formal red or green centerpiece?"

"Very pretty," Sylvia agreed, although she wasn't sure it would suit her friend's happily cluttered farmhouse. Sue and her apple farmer husband, Frank, still had three teenaged boys at home, so visitors were more likely to find a football on her dinner table than a formal centerpiece.

"Oh, look at this darling snowman fabric!" Lila exclaimed, picking up a bolt of red cotton with whimsical snowmen characters tumbling across it. She unrolled a length of the fabric and smiled with delight. "These happy fellows will make the perfect quilt for the little boy a young couple from my church just adopted. What do you think?"

"He'll be crazy about it," Anne Brown, the Post's energetic sales clerk agreed. "Any child would love those bright colors. Shall I cut it for you?"

Lila nodded then pulled another bolt from the display. This one featured a white line drawing of a Nativity scene repeated across a royal blue background. "And give me enough of this one to make a table runner for Pastor Steve."

She turned toward her friends and confided. "Every time

I quilt a gift for someone in the church, our pastor complains that I've never made a quilt for him."

"Oh, Lila, I don't know if that's such a good idea." Ellen frowned. She and Lila attended the same church, so she was well acquainted with the cleric in question. "Steve seems to get a real kick out of complaining about your quilts. This could ruin his fun."

"I know." The older woman gave them an impish grin. "In fact, I'm going to make a big production and give it to him at Christmas services when the church will be nice and full. That should put a cork in it for a while."

"Lila, that's plain naughty. You'd better hope Santa isn't listening," Anne teased then went off to cut the fabric.

Sylvia laughed with the others then wandered away to browse the regular selection of fabric. She had an idea in mind for her next project and was eager to get started. It would be a large wall hanging based on a very old pattern she'd seen at a quilt show when she and Dave were first married—the same quilt show that had ultimately brought her to The Stitching Post. The design, called the Calico Heart, was composed entirely of individual squares and triangles or half-squares. The pieces were assembled in rows then stacked to form heart shapes. Sylvia planned to machine sew the hearts, which would be much faster than doing it all by hand. When all the blocks were completed, she'd add the more time-consuming hand quilting to give it that beautiful, old-fashioned look.

Each block of the wall hanging would represent a destination she and Dave would visit on their travels. She envisioned the wall hanging done in rich jewel tones to coordinate with the furnishings in their den. She planned to use scraps of her favorite cranberry and red calico prints to make the heart in the central block. When it was assembled, she'd use gold floss to embroider the name of their first destination. It might be fun to add the date of their visit, too. She'd have to ask Dave what he thought of that idea. He had a good eye for design—a talent inherited by all their kids—and she always liked to get his opinion on her various quilt projects.

They'd both always loved this Calico Heart design. In fact, Dave had even carved a necklace for her with the heart pattern for her their first Valentine's Day together. She'd worn it almost every day until the hanging bale wore through. After that, she'd made a small pouch for the heart and always tucked it into her purse or pocket. Now, she patted the front pocket of her jeans and smiled at the familiar reminder of Dave's affection.

This would be so much fun.

The calico fabric for the first heart of the quilt was in her bag this evening. It would be the central block of the wall hanging, and Sylvia planned to use one of the shop's rotary cutters and mats to carefully cut the small squares so they would be nice and even. She knew in her head the order in which she'd lay out the squares. She'd pictured it for years. The travel destination was picked out for the main heart, too. It had been decided on several years ago, and she had been gathering brochures about the place ever since. Every time she opened the drawer in her sewing table, the name would jump out at her.

Mackinac Island.

Chapter Four

"I don't want to go."

"What?"

Puzzled, Sylvia put down the travel section of the Sunday paper she'd been reading at the kitchen table and turned toward the breakfast bar where Dave was assembling sandwiches with studious care. "What do you mean, honey?"

"Just what I said. I don't want to go."

"But we've been planning this for ages–"

"No, Syl. *You've* been planning it."

"Okay." She nodded. "Granted, I've done most of the research, but it's been based on the things we've talked about. Things you've always enjoyed: history, archaeology, and—" She laughed and drew air quotes with two fingers of each hand. "Plenty of photo ops."

"I don't need to travel hundreds of miles for those things. I can see them on TV and be a lot more comfortable."

"Come on, honey, you know that's not the same as being there in person."

"Close enough," he said, carefully spreading the mayo on a slice of bread so the condiment covered it from crust to crust.

Sylvia leaned back in the chair and stared at him. "Who are you, and what have you done with my husband?"

He frowned. The expression changed his pleasant features into a stern mask that suddenly reminded her of his late Grandfather Beaumont.

"Not funny," he muttered in a tone that sounded eerily like his grandfather's, too.

"It wasn't meant to be," she replied then busied herself gathering up the newspaper and folding it to control her irritation. She took a deep breath then tried again. "Honey, when we young and the kids were small, you told me you'd always wanted to travel. That you'd never had the chance when you were young. We promised we'd see the world together one day. When the kids were grown, we were retired, and we had enough money saved."

"That was then." He picked up the slice of bread, checking to make sure it was properly coated. Apparently, it passed scrutiny; he set it down and picked up the next slice. "I've changed."

"So have I. It's evident every time I look in my mirror and see another new wrinkle or another gray hair," she teased, trying to lighten her husband's mood.

"That's not what I mean." He laid down the bread and knife and finally looked at her.

A chill crept up Sylvia's spine, warning her she wasn't going to like what her husband was about to say.

"I can't do it, Sylvia," he began. "I just can't justify wasting all that money on a trip."

"How can you call traveling a waste?"

He sighed. "We've been over this."

He picked up the knife again and scooped more mayo from the jar. "There's no reason we *need* to go to Mackinac Island. Yes, the beaches are lovely, and yes, the fudge is good. But we have beautiful beaches less than thirty minutes from here, and you make killer fudge. So, we don't need to spend hundreds of dollars to be cooped up in a bus with a bunch of smelly senior citizens for hours, just so we can sleep in an overpriced hotel and shop for souvenirs we don't need."

Sylvia counted to ten. At least, she thought she did. She might have missed a number or two, but she was far too angry to start again. "Smelly senior citizens? That's a pretty rude bit of stereotyping, Dave. Especially since neither of us is getting any younger, pal."

Dave had the grace to look embarrassed, but didn't seem inclined to drop the argument. "That's not the point," he muttered, shoving the knife into the mayo jar with such force that it clinked loudly against the glass side.

"So explain it to me." She sat back in the chair and crossed her arms.

"I can't justify it, Sylvie," he said, using the pet name he'd given her in their early days together. "It's way too much money to spend. And for what? Just to sleep for a night in some hotel where Christopher Reeves once made a movie? No thanks, I can see the place on video."

"Honey, it's not just that. The whole island is listed as a national historic landmark. You've always been such a history buff. I thought you'd enjoy visiting places like Fort Mackinac, Mission Church, and—"

"Stop!" He leaned across the counter toward her. "Sylvia, listen to me. I don't want to go to Mackinac Island."

"Okay, then where do you want to go?"

He shrugged. "I don't need to go anywhere."

"I know you don't *need* to go anywhere," she said, trying to hide her exasperation. "But I want to go somewhere. So, where will you agree to go?"

"I don't want to go *anywhere*!" he said, banging his fist on the counter. "Why the blazes can't you understand that?"

Sylvia wasn't sure which shocked her more: his words or his uncharacteristic show of temper. She could count on one hand—and still have fingers left over—the number of times they'd ever argued during their marriage. Neither she nor Dave liked to raise their voices or lose their tempers. Sure, they'd had their disagreements, but they'd always approached things calmly and looked for acceptable compromises. Now, Dave's angry features made it quite clear that compromise wouldn't be an option.

To be honest, she didn't feel much like compromising either at that moment. She was angry, *very* angry. This was her future, too; the retirement she'd worked for just as hard as he had. For most of their marriage, she'd taught college-level math classes and had made a good wage but had lived frugally in order to contribute to their savings. Over the years, when her colleagues had talked about their plans for summer vacations and foreign excursions, Sylvia had comforted herself with the knowledge that her time would come, too, when she and Dave retired. It was why they'd planned to retire early, so they'd still be young enough and healthy enough to visit the places they wanted to see. Now, suddenly, Dave wanted to take all of that away from her.

"Okay, I understand you've decided you suddenly don't want to go anywhere. But what am I supposed to do? Stay here and watch you vegetate? I've been waiting all my life for the chance to travel and see some of this great world of ours. Good grief, I'd be glad just to see more of our state. Do you realize I've never been further than forty miles from our front door."

"Come on, it hasn't been that bad..."

"Dave, I've been taking care of a household since I was twelve years old."

"So, you helped out at home and ran a few errands for your parents. That's not unusual. Most people have done that."

"No, Dave. I did it all!"

She sighed. "You never really knew me back then. After all, you were two years ahead of me in high school, and we didn't start dating until I was in college. By then my mom and dad were both gone, and it seemed disrespectful to them to talk about those years."

"I know you didn't like talking about your family. I figured you had painful memories about losing them so suddenly—I could understand that since I lost my folks suddenly, too."

"It was more than that," Sylvia said then paused to take a breath. She hated talking about those days, about her mother's odd behavior. If people knew the whole truth about her mother, Sylvia worried that they might wonder if she would turn out the same way, too. After all, she shared the same genes. By the time she and Dave started dating several years after her parent's death, it had been easier to just put it behind her. She knew she should have told him, but it had been easier to bury the past with her parents. Now, she needed to open up about what happened and make her husband understand why she'd always avoided talking about her childhood and had changed the subject whenever anyone brought it up.

"Dave, when I tutored you in high school and always had to rush away afterwards, it wasn't because I had a hot date or because I wanted to meet friends. I had to rush home so I could take care of my mother. I did all the errands, all the stops to the dry cleaners or the hardware store, all the grocery shopping. Mom…Mom didn't like to go out."

"I'd hardly call running errands going out," Dave dismissed. "Those are necessities. We might not like them, but we have to do them."

"Mom couldn't."

"Couldn't?"

Sylvia nodded. "It started when I was still in grade school. Mom suddenly stopped going to church and to her various club meetings. Then she stopped even going outside to visit her friends. It got so she never left the house." Sylvia stopped and stared off in space for a moment, collecting herself. She'd buried that part of her past so deeply, she wasn't sure she could talk about it even to Dave. Would he think her mother had been crazy, or worse, wonder if *his wife* was?

"Mom didn't go to my school plays or to parent-teacher conferences. She didn't even go to my eighth grade graduation. At first, Dad made excuses, but after a while, he just seemed to accept it and relied on me to fill in for her."

"But she was sick, wasn't she?" Dave pulled out a chair and sat down beside her. "I remember you said she'd died when you were in high school. Before you started classes at Grand Valley."

Sylvia nodded. "Mom was agoraphobic—or at least I assume she was. No doctor ever diagnosed her. That would have meant she'd have to leave the house, and she wouldn't do that. Dad and I begged her to get help. He even made an appointment for her once, but she refused to keep it. The mere thought of going out the door gave her horrible anxiety attacks."

"What did she do all day? Did she have hobbies? Read? Sew? Watch TV?"

Sylvia shook her head. "Mom cleaned. And then she'd clean again. There was never a speck of dust in our house. Everything had a specific spot, and heaven help you if you moved something. Thinking about it, I guess Mom probably was OCD, too."

"My grandmother—my mom's mother—was kind of like that before she died. She always complained about the way my mother kept our house. I was really young, but I remember Mom would clean for days before one of Grandma's visits, trying to make sure the house and yard were perfect. But Grandma always found something wrong, a dust bunny in the far corner of the linen closet or a wilted carrot in the garden. Something she could disapprove of. The much anticipated visits always seemed to end with Mom in tears."

"Your poor mom," Sylvia said. Since Dave's parents had

been killed in a plane crash just a few months before his tenth birthday, she knew his grandmother's behavior had to have been pretty awful to make such lasting impression on him.

"Luckily, Dad was there to make light of the situation," Dave responded, dredging up a little smile. "Grandma died a year or so before my folks, so I don't know if she actually was OCD, but I think it's pretty likely."

He leaned toward his wife, his curiosity aroused. "Back to your mom, honey. She *never* went outside? Not ever, not at all?"

"At first, she did. Mom would go into our yard to work in her garden. It was always the nicest one in the neighborhood. You would have liked it," Sylvia said, referring to his fondness for gardening. "Mom spent hours out there planting, weeding, cultivating. She had a huge plot of vegetables. What we didn't use for the table, she canned. That's how I learned to do it."

"Then what happened?"

Sylvia clenched her hands together to hide their trembling. "The anxiety and agoraphobia got worse. By the time I was a junior, it had reached the point where she was terrified to even answer the door—or the phone. One day, in my senior year, I came home late from school and found her on the kitchen floor, unconscious. She'd had a major heart attack. The EMTs rushed her to the hospital, but she didn't make it.

Choking back the lump that had formed in her throat, she continued. "My dad was devastated. I think he'd always pretended to himself that Mom was just tired, that she'd wake up one day and be better again. When she died, he had to face the fact of how sick she'd been. He blamed himself for not insisting she see a doctor. He didn't sleep, didn't eat. About a month after Mom's death, he was driving home late one night and apparently fell asleep at the wheel. His car veered into the other lane and..."

"Oh, Syl! You poor baby. That must have been horrible

for you," Dave said. He wrapped his arms around her and pulled her over to his lap. "Honey, why did you never tell me?"

Sylvia bit her bottom lip. "I've always blamed myself for not coming home on time, Dave. If I'd been there when she had the heart attack and had called the EMTs sooner, maybe she and Dad both might—"

"Shh," he soothed, kissing the top of her head. "Don't think that way, honey. You were just a kid. Their deaths weren't your fault. What happened to your mom was tragic. There are treatments and medicines that could have helped her. It wasn't your fault."

"But what if it happens to me?" she whispered. "What if I start acting like my mother?"

"Honey, that isn't going to happen. If you started feeling those fears, you'd go to a doctor. We'd get you help, and we'd get through it together."

Sylvia wasn't sure it was as simple as that, but she leaned against his chest and let the comforting sound of his heartbeat fill her head. With his strong arms wrapped around her, she felt protected and loved. She dismissed her earlier irritation with him and leaned up to kiss the familiar curve of his jaw.

This was her strong and caring Dave.

Chapter Five

"And it can follow even the most complicated quilting templates," Anne said excitedly. The young clerk's eyes sparkled as she demonstrated the new Ansley long arm machine to The Stitching Post's quilting group.

"Look how beautiful that pattern is." Sue pointed to the elaborate scroll pattern Anne had made on a length of scrap material. "The stitches are so tiny and uniform."

Myra flipped up the free edge of the material and pointed to the circular pattern on the back side. "Just as pretty underneath, too," the shop owner said. "And the high-speed stitch regulator can do it all at a top speed of 3000 stitches a minute."

"Whoa, that's fast!" Theresa Donovan exclaimed, tucking a strand of auburn hair behind her ear. "Think how much time this baby could save you. I'll bet I can easily finish Ethan's bedspread with it in plenty of time for Christmas, as well as do the one for Kait."

Sylvia and Ellen exchanged an amused glance. Everything was always about saving time with their friend, Theresa. Tee operated a thriving one-woman real estate agency in town, headed the PTA at her children's school, baked cookies for their soccer teams, and sang in her church choir. Sylvia often felt tired just listening to the busy, single mother's schedule. But somehow, Tee always managed to fit in time for the quilt group on Tuesdays. Even if she did arrive late more often than not.

"Can you imagine how many quilts you could have finished in your lifetime using a machine like this, Lila?" the attractive business woman asked, turning to the older woman seated beside her. "You could have whipped up a quilt for your pastor years ago."

"What? And deprived him of all those opportunities to complain? Oh, I think not, my dear." The older woman scoffed, but her blue eyes twinkled merrily.

"I've been wondering," Sue said from her spot beside Sylvia. "Won't it spoil your pastor's fun, anyway...I mean when you give him the table runner?"

"Sure it will," the older woman conceded. "Until he realizes a table runner isn't the same as an actual quilt. Then, he'll start back up. I give him about two weeks."

After they shared a laugh, Ellen and Sue dug into their tote bags and pulled out fabric for the quilt blocks they were making. The calico squares Sylvia had cut for the first block of her travel quilt were in her tote bag, but she had little enthusiasm for piecing them together. Instead, she wandered over to join Anne, who was still seated at the long-arm quilting machine.

"You want to try it?" the young woman asked.

"Sure."

The two women switched places then Anne explained the various buttons on the twin control handles. The clerk helped Sylvia pick out a floral stitching template on the attached computer display then nodded for her to start. As soon as Sylvia pressed the throttle, the machine purred into action. Anne had made the operation look pretty effortless, but it took a good deal of concentration for Sylvia to get the knack and move the fabric through the machine at a steady pace. However, she quickly caught on and soon was operating the controls nearly as easily as Anne had done.

"That was fun," Sylvia said as she reached the end of the fabric remnant. "If no one else wants to try it, can I do another design pattern?"

Anne pointed to the rest of the quilters. "Everyone else is working on their projects, so go ahead. Which one do you want to try next?"

"You pick something," Sylvia said. "Nothing too complicated though."

"These looped hearts are nice," Anne said. "Wouldn't they be pretty for your Calico Heart wall hanging?"

Sylvia looked away and mumbled something noncommittal as she keyed in the heart template.

"How's it coming?"

"Fine. This computer pad is really easy to work."

The clerk chuckled. "Yes it is, but I meant your travel quilt. I haven't seen you working on it lately."

"Oh, that. Not so good."

"What's up? Is the design off?"

Sylvia shrugged then started the machine again. But this time, she couldn't seem to find the right rhythm. Her pattern ended up resembling a string of deflated balloons rather than a row of looped hearts. Frustrated, she released the throttle. "It's not the design. It's Dave."

Anne snagged the nearest empty chair and pulled it closer. Sitting down, she leaned toward Sylvia and pretended to fiddle with the quilter's computer screen. In a soft voice that wouldn't carry, she asked, "Is there anything I can do to help?"

"Thanks, but I don't think so." Sylvia sighed. "I just can't believe him lately. He's behaving like a totally different person than the man I married."

"Nobody stays the same for twenty-six years."

"Thirty if you count the four years we dated, too."

"There you go!" Anne chuckled. "I'm sure Dave sometimes wonders what happened to the girl he married, too."

Sylvia frowned, considering that.

She didn't think she'd changed that much. Sure there were physical differences. Bearing three children did things to a woman's body—and she'd never been too diligent about exercise—but she'd only gone up a single dress size since her high school days. However, she had noticed a few more strands of gray in her hair recently, and the fine lines around her eyes had gotten a good deal deeper. It was different with men. Sean Connery and Richard Gere were perfect examples. Gray hair made them look more handsome and distinguished. Women, on the other hand, just looked old when they got gray. Was Dave embarrassed by the changes in her as she'd aged? Was that why he didn't want to travel with her?

"Are you okay?" Sue asked.

Sylvia blinked and realized some of the others had noticed her sitting motionless by the quilting machine. She forced a smile, not wanting her friends to worry.

"I'm fine. Just daydreaming of all the things I could make with a machine like this."

She returned to her seat in the quilt circle and picked up her bag. It had been a gift from Dave, the Christmas she'd first begun quilting. From the outside it looked almost like a small overnight suitcase, but inside, there were compartments for her tools: scissors, thread, needles, quilt patterns, fabric cutter, and cutting mat. There was also plenty of room to carry the fabric and supplies for several projects. She started to reach for the plastic bag holding the red and cranberry calico squares she'd cut for the center of her travel quilt then stopped. Instead, she pulled out the fabric for the scrapbook cover she was making Lynne and Ron for Christmas.

"Not working on your travel quilt?" Sue tilted her head and looked curiously at the project in Sylvia's lap.

"I just don't feel like it tonight. I thought I'd work on the cover for Lynne's photo album."

Her friend pushed back a strand of hair that had worked its way loose from her ponytail. She anchored the dishwater brown strand behind her ear before continuing. "That happens sometime to me, too. It's why I always have several projects going at once. It drives Frank nuts."

"I imagine so," Sylvia remarked as she threaded a needle with a strand of sturdy thread.

Free-spirited Sue often bickered with her more regimented husband. They seemed to disagree on everything from her housekeeping to how they disciplined their three children. It was wonder the two opposites had remained married all these years. Sylvia lowered her hands to her lap as a sudden thought struck her. *Are Dave and I any different than Sue and Frank?* Sure, she and her husband seldom argued, but they certainly looked at life differently.

She jabbed her needle into the scrapbook cover with a bit more force than necessary. His recent refusal to go on the bus trip was a perfect example. *Who on earth would possibly believe watching a travelogue is just as good as visiting somewhere in person?* She jabbed the needle into the material again. *Nobody, that's who!*

"Is Dave still being difficult about going on your bus trip?" Ellen asked, pointing at Sylvia's needle.

"Or a car trip or plane or train."

"Maybe he has other ideas for your retirement," Tee suggested. The thirty-something dynamo looked up from the dinosaur she was tracing for her son's quilt. "Maybe he's planning a second career. Or maybe he's decided he doesn't want to retire at all. Lots of folks change their minds in these tough times."

Several of the others agreed, and the conversation turned

to people they knew who'd lost their jobs or found new ones in Michigan's weakened economy. Sylvia breathed a sigh of relief. There was nothing worse than having problems aired in public, as her father used to say. Besides, she was certain this was just a passing phase with Dave. Surely, her dear husband would soon change his tune. After all, they'd been planning on taking early retirements for ages, and he knew how she'd collected all those brochures on places she wanted to see. Destinations in Michigan as well as fascinating places much farther away. Like the Smithsonian, Mt. Rushmore, the Texas Quilt Museum. Even Disney World.

But what if Dave no longer wanted to retire? She frowned. If he kept working, there wouldn't be any fun destinations for her to embroider on a travel quilt. Nor any quilt for that matter.

What would she do with her time? She'd already retired from Grand Valley, and the university had hired a professor to replace her. Fall classes would start in just a few weeks, so it was much too late to apply for another position or put in resumes at other local colleges.

She sighed. Oh well, she'd always wished she'd had more time to do the things she liked: reading, quilting, canning. It looked like she'd have plenty of time to do all of them now.

Especially since travel doesn't look like it will be an option any longer.

At nine-thirty, the women started to pack their projects to take home. Myra stood at the cash register, ringing up last minute items some of the quilters needed. Anne helped a few of the others with their last minute fabric purchases. Sylvia carefully stowed her own supplies in her case then called good-bye to her friends.

She had almost reached the door when she heard a quiet voice calling her name. She turned to find Lila behind her.

"Walk me out to the car, will you?" the older woman asked.

"Of course," Sylvia agreed quickly, noticing the odd expression on her friend's normally animated features. "Are you okay? Let me carry your bag for you."

"I'm fine dear," Lila assured her, adjusting her shoulder tote. She didn't say anything more until they left the shop, then she turned to Sylvia.

"I couldn't help but hear you talking to Ellen and Sue earlier. I know you're upset with Dave, my dear, but you know, there are a lot worse things in a husband than not wanting to travel. Dave is faithful to you, and he's never lifted a hand to you or the kids. He's been a good husband and father. I'm sure the two of you can work out any other differences."

"You're right, and I agree." Sylvia sighed. "It's just that we've looked forward to this time for so long. We've made so many plans over the years. Or at least I thought we had. Now, Dave says it was all my planning not his."

A sad expression clouded the older woman's face. "Men can be so obtuse. I used to rant and rave when my Marvin didn't want to go anywhere. I called him an old stick in the mud. But, now, I'd give almost anything to see him sitting in his recliner, just smoking his pipe and reading his paper."

Sylvia felt her face burn. Lila hadn't been criticizing her, but the woman's gentle reminder still hit home. "I'm sorry. I probably sounded pretty selfish this evening. I love Dave, and I know I'm lucky to be married to him.

She reached in her pocket and pulled out the pouch with the small wooden heart she always carried. She handed it to her friend. "Dave made this for me a long time ago."

"Why, it's a carved Calico Heart."

Sylvia nodded, rubbing her thumb over the pattern carved into the heart's face. "We saw a quilt made like this at the show where I first met you, and I fell in love with the design. We were newlyweds and couldn't afford to buy the quilt—I doubt we could afford it even now—so Dave carved this pendant for me. I wore it every day until the bale finally wore through a few years ago. Since then, I always have it in my pocket or purse."

"It's a keeper," her friend remarked, handing the heart back to her. "Just like Dave is."

"I know. I just wish I knew what was going on in his head..."

"You know, Theresa could be right. David might just be worrying about retiring in these economic times."

"It's possible. Dave has always fretted about expenses. His grandfather drilled fiscal responsibility into his head since he was just a kid. 'Waste not, want not,' and all those platitudes. Dave's always worried that our savings might not be enough." She stopped and suddenly smiled. "I'll bet he is just afraid our traveling might jeopardize our future needs."

"Most likely," Lila agreed.

"Wow," Sylvia mused. "Now, I wish I hadn't already retired. If I'd kept working, I could have started my own savings account and surprised Dave with the extra funds for some fun trips. That might have eased his mind a little bit about the cost of traveling. Poor Dave, he always frets about rainy days."

"Why don't you look for another job? You're still young enough to find a position. You probably wouldn't even need to work full-time."

Sylvia clapped her hands in delight.

"Lila, I could kiss you! That might be the perfect solution. Dave can hardly object about spending the money for a vacation if I earn it myself."

Chapter Six

Sylvia scowled at the newspaper's Help Wanted section spread across her kitchen table as if her disapproval might change the ads on the pages. There had to be something that a woman with her education and career experience could do on a temporary basis.

For the last week, she'd combed the ads every night, looking for a position. Every morning, she called to inquire on the listings that looked the most promising. So far, nothing had panned out. It wasn't like she was looking for some high-paid executive position; she was perfectly willing to do manual labor or fast food work. But even those positions were full time. The few temporary jobs she'd heard about required a lot more computer skills than she possessed, or else they were further away than she wanted to travel. Part of the problem was the time of year. Kids on summer break had snapped up most of the local part-time jobs. Several places she'd called had asked her to call back in the fall, when the students went back to school.

She sighed and folded up the paper. She'd look again tomorrow. Something was bound to come up. If not, she might have to check with a temp agency. Hopefully, they handled clients who weren't computer savvy.

Now, it was time to get supper ready. She wanted to have it ready to put on the table when Dave got home, so she could get to The Stitching Post on time. Just as she rose from her chair, the phone rang. A glance at the caller ID told her it was Dave, calling from his office.

"Hi, honey. I wanted to call and let you know I'm going to be late coming home tonight."

"Is everything okay?"

"Yeah, just some reports to finish," he told her. "But I know it's your quilting night, so I didn't want you to wait for me. Go ahead without me. I'll grab a bite on the way home."

"Okay. Maybe I'll do the same. I lost track of time and was just starting to think about supper now."

"Did you get caught up in some soap?" Dave teased. "One General Restless Life to Turn?"

She laughed at his familiar joke. "Hardly. I was looking at the Help Wanted Ads and forgot about the time."

There was silence for a moment. "You're looking for a job? You just retired."

"I know, honey. I'm just looking for something temporary. And part-time."

"Why?"

"For extras...like vacations."

"I see."

Sylvia winced at the icy disapproval the two words carried, but refused to let him deter her. "Since your main objection to us traveling seems to be the expense, I thought I could help out by earning the extra we need. That way, it wouldn't take anything from our savings or affect the budget you set up with our pension checks. This would all be extra money, right?"

When he didn't reply, she figured he was already processing the new idea and crunching the numbers.

"Thanks for letting me know about working late, honey. I'll see you tonight after quilting."

****

Dave fought the urge to slam down the phone and set it down carefully instead. His team members might wonder why their normally unflappable manager was suddenly throwing a temper tantrum. That wouldn't have been cool. His entire career he'd been Mr. Calm and Levelheaded. His management considered David Miller to be the go-to guy in any crisis. But right now, he felt neither calm nor levelheaded. In fact, his wife's words made him want to throw something.

He couldn't believe Sylvia was this determined to travel. He'd expected her to kick back and enjoy being retired. She would have the time to quilt, have coffee with friends, maybe even volunteer a little at that nursing home where she donated the lap quilts she and her friends made. He certainly hadn't expected her to look for a job. What would he do if she found one? He could hardly dictate how she spent the money.

Blast it! How could he have forgotten the promises they'd made each other so long ago? When she used to talk about the places she wanted to visit someday, her face had lit up and her blue eyes had sparkled with excitement. He'd been so caught up in the magic of her fantasies that he'd forgotten his shame at being left a penniless orphan and his grandfather's dire warnings about the frivolous expense and countless dangers inherent in travel.

Syl's excitement had made him forget that he and his siblings would have been left at the mercy of the welfare system if his grandfather hadn't stepped in. At least, he and Bill would have been; Muriel had already been a junior at Michigan State at the time. But she certainly wouldn't have been able to graduate and go on for her master's without grandfather's support.

Grandfather had been good to them. Grandmother had died a year before his parents, so Grandfather had had to be both mother and father to Dave and his siblings. True, it had been Grandfather's housekeeper who always saw to Dave's needs, taking him to school, to doctor appointments, and to his sports practices. But Grandfather had been there at dinnertime, asking about his day, checking his report cards, and admonishing him for buying the latest record album.

"Popular artists change every week," he'd scolded. "It's ridiculous to buy their records when you can listen to the same songs for free on the radio. Do you want to end up broke like your parents?"

It was odd, but Dave couldn't remember his parents being poor. He remembered a rambling home in Grand Haven, lots of laughter, family skiing vacations in the winter and fishing with his dad in the summertime. He recalled noisy birthday parties, hours spent in the tree house his dad had built, and wonderful family dinners. Grandfather had later explained that those memories were nothing but illusions. His father's careless spending had put the family in debt and left Dave and his siblings in dire straits.

When Dave had started dating Sylvia, it had been like finding sunlight at the end of a dark tunnel. He'd been attracted to her the moment he'd heard her laughter floating across the crowded cafeteria. But he'd been a senior, and the bubbly little sophomore hadn't seemed interested. She'd never attended his games or any of the school dances. Of course, now he knew why, but he hadn't had a clue back then. So he'd dated others and eventually had gone off to college.

When he'd heard that same laugh again, years later, in the bookstore at Grand Valley, he'd nearly fallen on his face hurrying over to say hello. They'd been together ever since. When she'd accepted his proposal and the modest engagement ring he'd been able to afford, it had been the happiest day of his life. Dave vowed to make a good life for her and whatever children they'd have.

He felt like he'd fulfilled his promise. He'd worked hard and had made a good living. They had a nice, mortgage-free home, the kids had good educations, and he and Sylvia had a healthy nest egg built up for a comfortable retirement. He hadn't been as unbending as his grandfather about it either. The kids had had MP3 players, cell phones and clothes that were comparable to what their friends had. But they'd also been taught the value of a dollar. All of them had held down jobs during their high school and college years, and they'd learned to save part of every paycheck for a rainy day. After all, one never knew what was going to happen from one day to the next.

So why did Sylvia want to risk all that now? With so many travel programs available on video and TV, there was no need to visit those destinations. A person could sit in the safety and comfort of their home and enjoy a better tour than they'd probably get if they were there in person. After all, the media had access to places the average Dave and Sylvia Miller couldn't go.

Why on earth couldn't his wife realize that?

Chapter Seven

"I can't tell you how thrilled Ethan's summer school teacher is with his progress," Tee told the quilt group a couple of weeks later. "Just one hour with Sylvia, and fractions suddenly make sense to him."

Sylvia waved away the compliment. "Young boys quickly get the idea when you use their favorite pie to demonstrate the difference between one fourth and one eighth. I assure you, it works even faster with teenagers."

"You're too modest, Sylvia. I don't know what we would have done without you. Even with extra summer school classes, Ethan just wasn't getting it. I was afraid I'd have to hold him back a year," Tee confided. "But now, he's actually eager for school to start again."

"I'm glad I could help. It was fun, and it gave me something to do with my free time."

Ellen looked at her friend over the top of the magnifying glasses she wore whenever she quilted. "Still no luck on the job front?"

Sylvia shook her head and tacked a last bit of lace on Lynne's scrapbook cover. "No, but the burger place on Wilson told me they would probably have a couple of openings when the kids go back to school."

"Good grief, Sylvia!" Tee exclaimed in horror. "Please tell me you are not seriously thinking about flipping burgers."

"Actually, I'm hoping to work the counter or the drive-thru. I'm not too proud to ask 'do you want fries with that?' if it means I can earn the money I want for my travel fund."

The younger woman's beautifully-cut auburn hair fanned out around her then settled back perfectly in place when she shook her head. "You don't need to push fries, Sylvia. You could easily be making four times as much an hour."

"I'm sure I could," Sylvia agreed then quirked an eyebrow. "But I don't think Dave would like it if I started my own phone sex line."

Lila laughed so hard at the unexpected comment that she snorted. "Just be glad I wasn't drinking tea, young lady," she scolded, "or you'd have been wearing it."

Tee laughed along with the others then grew serious again. "What I had in mind, Syl, is a bit less—um—adventurous than phone sex," she said. "You know, I'm head of the parent-teacher group at my kids' school, and I've heard a lot of the parents—teachers, too—complain about the shortage of good tutors. If you wanted to offer your services, I could hook you up with as many students as you wanted with just a few phone calls."

"Are you kidding me?" Sylvia leaned forward eagerly. "You'd do that for me?

"Of course, I would, silly. Look how you helped me with Ethan. I can recommend you first hand. Just let me know what you'd charge, and I'll start making calls."

"What a perfect idea!" Sylvia clapped her hands with delight. "I could tutor children after school and be finished before Dave came home for supper."

"Of course there is one condition," Tee said.

"What's that?" Sylvia asked. "Do I need a background

check or bonding or something?"

Her friend shrugged. "I'm not sure. Maybe. The school office can tell us for certain. My condition is that you have to agree to let me pay you for tutoring Ethan as your first student."

"Now you're being silly. I was glad to do it. That's what friends are for."

"Syl, honey, listen to me," the realtor instructed. "If you listed your house with me, and I sold it for you, you'd expect to pay me a commission, right?"

"Of course, I would."

"Well, this is the same thing. This is your business."

"No, I couldn't—" Sylvia started to protest but stopped when Lila gave her a sharp nudge in the side.

"Don't be stupid, my dear. This is perfect for you. Besides, where else are you going to find a job that won't interfere with our quilt group?"

Chapter Eight

"I'm not going."

"What? Why not? This isn't going to take a cent from our retirement account, Dave. It's all extra money. Money we can spend to have fun or travel or do extra things! There's more than enough to pay for our bus fares, hotel accommodations, and still have spending money on the island, too."

"It doesn't matter how we pay for it. It's still a waste of money. If you want to go, fine. Like you said, you earned it. But I won't enjoy myself spending money on something so frivolous."

"Frivolous?" Sylvia hated the way her voice rose, but she couldn't seem to stop herself from screeching. "How on earth can you call this trip frivolous? When you used to help the kids study, you would always point to places like this on the map and tell them all about it. About how important it was for a person to know their history, and—"

"And I was able to teach them all about American history without having to visit all those places, Sylvia. I didn't need to go then, and I certainly don't need to go now."

Knowing that arguing further was useless, she stuck the

brochure for Mackinac Island into the pile she held. Leaning back in the chair, she took a deep breath to calm her racing heart, and let the August sunshine warm her face. *What had happened to the travel plans they'd dreamed about? Why was Dave behaving like this?*

He had his back to her, ignoring her as he carefully sanded the piece of wood in front of him. She watched how his muscles bunched then relaxed beneath his t-shirt as he worked. His shoulders were still as broad as they'd been back in his football days, she thought with a smile.

The smell of fresh-cut wood tickled her nose. Dave had always liked to work with wood, but this new project was far more ambitious than the small pieces he used to carve for relaxation. This time, he was making a set of chairs for the patio. He'd bought the wood the week before and had spent several days meticulously measuring and marking. The old adage warned to "measure twice and cut once," but Dave had probably measured every piece at least a dozen times before making the first cut. Now, they lay on the patio floor, waiting to be sanded then assembled.

Sylvia frowned. This new hobby of his was supposed to be relaxing not stressful. But her husband seemed tenser than ever as he worked on each piece. Of course, Dave never understood her passion for quilting, either. Maybe she should just be happy he'd found a new hobby to occupy his time. But he didn't need to ignore her.

Irritated, she tapped the bundle of travel brochures against the arm of her lawn chair and pursed her lips, thinking. Dave had said he didn't want to go on the trip and had almost dared her to go by herself. Time to put that idea to the test.

"I figured you wouldn't want to go on the Mackinac Island trip," she said to his back. "So I called the travel agency this morning, and put a deposit down on a different excursion for myself. I'm all set for an extended trip to the South Pole," she fibbed, waiting for his reaction. When none came, she continued. "I should get there just in time to see the migration of the penguins."

"Mmm-hmm."

"I'll be downstairs getting out the luggage if you need me," she announced, heading back into the house. She detoured to her sewing room and tossed the brochures on the desk before going down to the basement.

The luggage set hid behind a pile of sports equipment like a naughty child avoiding an angry parent. The kids had used a piece or two for various school trips, but the family had never used the whole set since they'd never gone anywhere together. The last time Sylvia recalled any of it being used was when Lynne had been a high school senior and had gone to a band competition in Indiana. She and Dave hadn't been able to go since they'd both had to work. Now, as she moved aside three pairs of skis, two bowling balls, a tent, and assorted backpacks, Sylvia reminded herself that it was long past time for the kids to come and collect all their gear.

She tugged the dusty suitcases from their corner and looked them over. Luckily, they weren't in too bad a shape. She examined the largest piece with a critical eye, rotating it to check for rips or damage. It looked okay. The zippers still worked; the wheels still rolled, and the handle mechanisms retracted only a bit stiffly. The case was basic black in a tight-woven fabric. It wasn't very feminine, but it would serve the purpose once it was cleaned off. The smaller pieces, having been nested inside the largest case, were in almost new condition.

Sylvia selected a medium piece then zipped the others back inside the big case. This time, she stored the luggage against the wall near the washer and dryer so they'd be handy. She might not need more than one piece this time, but she didn't want to have to dig them out the next time.

As she headed up the stairs with the case in one hand, an

enraged bellow suddenly boomed from the direction of the back patio.

"The South Pole? What in the blazes do you mean you're going to the South Pole?"

Chapter Nine

"Are you going to work on your travel quilt tonight?" Lila asked when Sylvia joined the group at The Stitching Post the next evening.

The older woman's question didn't surprise Sylvia. The previous week, she had shared with the group that she'd already managed to save more than enough money to pay for the first bus excursion for her and Dave. But she didn't want to talk about that just now.

"Not tonight," Sylvia said. She finger-combed her thick, black hair, lifting it off her neck. "Boy, it sure is hot this evening."

"Supposed to get hotter the rest of the week, too," Ellen commented as she and Sue pulled their chairs closer.

"Well, you know what they say," Lila said. "It's not the heat, it's..."

"The humidity," her friends answered in unison.

"And we've got plenty of that, too." Sylvia commented.

"What are you working on tonight?" Sue pointed to the pale blue squares Sylvia had pulled from her tote.

"I need to finish the baby quilt I'm making for Lynne..."

"Lynne is expecting?" Lila exclaimed. "Why didn't you tell us before tonight?"

"Congratulations!" Ellen and Sue chimed.

"No, no!" Sylvia laughed. "I'm not going to be a grandma quite yet. This is for one of her co-workers. Lynne started it but just hasn't had time to work on it, so I said I'd finish it for her."

"What about your travel quilt?" Ellen asked. "I thought you'd be eager to start on it now that you have the money for your trip."

"This needs to be done first," Sylvia replied. "The baby is due in September. Besides, I don't think I'm going to need the travel quilt for a while yet."

"Why not?"

"It's Dave...of course." Sylvia sighed and pulled out her needle and thread. "I can't believe him. He's like a totally different person from the man I married."

Sylvia muttered as she tried to thread her needle. The blasted thread refused to cooperate, and she missed the eye for the third time. Her friends murmured sympathetically then bent to their work. Sylvia again tried without success to thread her needle. Frustrated, she jabbed it into her pile of fabric and threw her hands in the air in disgust.

Ellen reached over and calmly picked up the needle and thread. She looped the length of thread, slipped it through the needle's eye then handed it back to her friend and said, "Here. Quilt. It will make you feel better."

Sylvia nodded and began to applique the colorful boats Lynne had already prepared on the pale blue backing. After a few moments, the rhythmic in-and-out motion of the needle soothed the tension from her muscles. Sylvia crossed her ankles and relaxed in her chair, losing herself in the simple pleasure of her craft.

"Sylvia?"

She looked up to find Lila studying her, a concerned look

on her face.

"Remember the conversation we had a few weeks ago about Dave?" the older woman asked.

"Yes, and you were right," Sylvia said. "I know Dave still worries about the money we spent on Lynne's wedding. But that's not the problem, Lila. We already had a nice amount set aside—ear-marked for each of the kids' college and weddings—and I stayed pretty much within our budget."

She stopped and bit her lip, forcing back the angry tears suddenly blurring her vision. "This trip wouldn't affect our finances, Lila. I made this money with my tutoring. It's all extra money. Not part of our household budget. I just don't understand Dave's attitude or why he's being so stubborn. And he refuses to discuss it.

"I really wanted this trip," she finished, brushing aside a tear.

Lilac patted her hand and gave her a gentle smile.

"I'm sorry," Sylvia apologized. "I know that sounds spoiled, and I should be grateful I have—"

"Nonsense, my dear," Lila interrupted. "You aren't being selfish at all. You know, Marvin never liked to travel, but I did. When we retired, he often preferred to stay home, but he encouraged me to go places without him. I found this group—Traveling Solo, it's called—that specialized in bus trips for singles. Not necessarily people who are widowed or unmarried, just people who travel alone for whatever their reasons. I had lots of fun and made so many lovely friends. We had some funny adventures, too. Things I might not have had if Marvin had come along," she confided with an impish grin.

"Really?" Tee looked up from her dinosaur quilt. "Tell us."

"Perhaps another time, dear. Right now, we need to concentrate on Sylvia's problem. Do you have any friends you can travel with?"

"Not really. Most of them have families at home, or they still have jobs."

"Then you need to contact my singles group," Lila said as if the matter were decided.

Sylvia's first reaction was to disagree. After all, she wasn't single; she had a husband, a husband she loved. Still, Lila had a point. If Dave refused to go anywhere, why should that stop her from following her dreams? If she didn't have to worry about trying to find a destination Dave would like, she could go literally anywhere she wanted. The options were endless.

Shoot, she could even go to see the penguin migration if she wanted.

Chapter Ten

"C'mon, Sylvia, either call the number or throw it away!"

Sylvia looked at the piece of paper sitting on her kitchen table and frowned. She'd already spent most of the morning sitting and staring at the seven digits written on it in Lila's somewhat shaky handwriting. She took a sip of her coffee and scolded herself for being so indecisive. Acting this wishy-washy was totally out of character for her. It was almost as if someone had taken over her body like in those bad sci-fi movies she hated. But then, lately, her life had seemed to resemble a bad sci-fi, one where the main characters seemed vaguely familiar but she wasn't quite able to name them.

No more. It was time to make a decision. She dragged the bulky, old-fashioned phone from the kitchen counter and set it in the middle of the table. After one last fortifying sip of coffee, Sylvia reached for the receiver. Just then, the phone suddenly emitted a shrill ring. Startled, she jerked back her hand as if she'd been attacked. But the phone merely rang a second time. Chuckling at her foolishness, she picked up the receiver and said hello.

"What's so funny?"

"Oh! Hi, Dave." Embarrassed to have been caught in her foolishness, she ignored his question. "What's up?"

"Just calling to tell you I just got scheduled into a late afternoon meeting. One of our corporate clients is coming in, and Roger wants all hands on deck. We'll probably go out to dinner, too. So it will probably be a late night."

"No problem. Lila asked me to go with her to a meeting tonight, so this will work out fine."

"Another quilting group?"

"No..." Sylvia crossed her fingers then plunged ahead. "It's a group for people who travel alone. Lila's been a member for a number of years now. She thought I might like to check it out."

Silence. Sylvia could almost feel ice crystal forming on the receiver.

"I mean, Lila knows you're busy at work and can't really travel right now," Sylvia rushed on, trying to fill the cold silence. "She thought I might like the group."

"I see," Dave replied. "Well, I guess I didn't need to worry about you being alone this evening since you already had plans."

"It wasn't like that. I hadn't decided—"

"Have a good time, Sylvia," he continued over her objections. "Talk to you later."

Sylvia frowned and hung up the phone, uncertain what to make of the odd conversation. Had Dave been irritated or relieved to learn of her plans? His words could have meant either. She shrugged. He had no right to be upset. After all, he'd been the one to suggest she go on a trip by herself.

"If he didn't mean it, he shouldn't have said it," she told the empty room then picked up the phone to call the number on Lila's paper.

****

"Welcome, welcome," a curvy brunette greeted when Sylvia arrived at the office of Traveling Solo that evening. "You must be new to the group. I'm Deanna, one of the tour directors."

"I'm Sylvia. My friend, Lila Haggerty, told me about your group, but she couldn't come with me this evening."

Deanna nodded and waved her toward a large conference room. "Any friend of Lila's is definitely welcome here. Please, make yourself at home while we wait for the others to arrive. There are plenty of drinks and refreshments. Get yourself something to eat and mingle a bit. That's what we're about here."

Sylvia didn't feel much like eating or socializing, but she went inside. Small clusters of people stood around, chatting easily, but Sylvia noticed there were also plenty of singles, both female and male, sitting by themselves. Some of them read, some did various types of needlework, and others just sat and looked around the room. She found a seat at the end of a row and settled in to wait for the meeting to start.

"Sylvia Miller? Is that you?"

Sylvia looked up at the sound of her name. A pleasantly plump woman headed in her direction, holding out her arms in greeting. Sylvia smiled and hurried to greet her former co-worker. Marcia Ames had retired from Grand Valley the previous year, and Sylvia hadn't seen her since.

"What a wonderful surprise. It's so good to see you, Marcia. What are you doing here?"

"I could ask the same," the woman said, dropping her purse on the chair next to Sylvia's then taking her by the arm. "But first, let's grab some refreshments—at my age, I never turn down an opportunity for free cake."

Arm in arm, they crossed the room, stopping to greet some of Marcia's friends. The woman seemed to know everyone they encountered and introduced so many people that Sylvia soon gave up trying to keep them all straight. But they were a cordial group, and Sylvia soon forgot her awkwardness at being there by herself. When they returned to their seats with their refreshments—a glass of tea for Sylvia and a piece of chocolate cake and coffee for Marcia—the two women settled in to catch up.

Marcia explained that her husband Eric had suffered a stroke shortly after retiring. Afterwards, he'd needed daily therapy and more care than she could have given, but Marcia hadn't wanted to put him in a nursing home. So, they'd sold their home and moved into a retirement community. It was the best of both worlds. They had their own apartment, but the facility also provided on-site therapy for those who needed it. In addition to the therapy room, there was also a gym and pool for all the residents to use. They were happy with the arrangement, but Eric knew how much Marcia loved to travel, so he encouraged her to take some little excursions without him. That was how she'd signed up with Traveling Solo.

"I've only made a couple of day trips with the group," Marcia confided, "but I never miss one of these monthly meetings. Everyone is so darned nice, and picking a destination for the next excursion is always a lot of fun."

"Where's the next one going?"

Marcia smiled happily and sat back in her seat. "Mackinac Island," she answered. "Can you imagine anywhere more perfect?"

Chapter Eleven

"—then bake for forty-five minutes," Lynne repeated. "Okay, that sounds easy, even for me."

Sylvia could imagine her daughter sitting at the table in the breakfast nook of her Heritage Hills home, with the phone on speaker mode so she could write down the instructions. "I should have done this before your wedding, Lynne. I could have run off copies of my recipe cards on the printer and saved you all the writing."

Lynne's laugh floated from the phone. "Are you kidding, Mom? You know how Ron loves your cooking. If I'd had your recipes, he would have expected me to cook every night. This way, it's always a treat when I make one of your specialties."

"You wouldn't have had to tell him."

"Mom!" Her daughter gasped in mock horror. "Are you suggesting I keep secrets from my sweet husband?"

Sylvia thought about that for all of a second. "No. It wouldn't have worked anyway. You never could keep secrets."

"I know. It's why you always took me Christmas shopping at the last moment. That way, there was at least a chance I might not spill the beans and tell Dad and the boys what I got them."

"Exactly! So how are you going to manage it this year?

"You mean you won't take me anymore?" Lynne pretended to sigh.

"I doubt you really want me to come along while you pick out Ron's sock and briefs."

"Boxers, Mom."

"T.M.I!" Sylvia laughed in the phone, enjoying the back-and-forth banter she and her daughter always shared.

"Like you haven't been washing men's underwear for more than a quarter of a century now."

"A quarter of a century? Good grief! That makes your father and me sound ancient."

"I refuse to comment," Lynne remarked then turned to a different subject. "What are you and Dad doing on Labor Day?"

"We really don't have anything much going on over the holiday. Since your brothers have made plans with some friends and aren't coming home, and you and Ron are heading to his folks' place, Dad and I will probably grill a couple of steaks."

"You should come with us. Mr. and Mrs. Cross have plenty of room."

"Can't, honey. Davis Andrew always has their company picnic on the Saturday before Labor Day, remember? That's the one thing we do have on our calendar for the weekend."

Lynne groaned. "How could I forget? It's always such a bundle of laughs. Forty-some bean counters arguing about the fastest route for the three-legged race."

"It's not that bad. Besides, your father is one of those bean counters."

"Isn't he ever going to retire?" Lynne asked. "I thought the two of you were going to do it at the same time, so you could travel and—"

"That was the plan, but there are a few bills we wanted to pay off first. Maybe he'll retire the end of the year. Or next spring."

"Are they bills from my wedding? Is that why Daddy doesn't feel like he can retire? Did you have to start tutoring to pay off my wedding?"

"No, no, not at all." Sylvia hurried to reassure her youngest. "We had money set aside for that, honey. It's just your father. You know how he is. He has his annual review coming up in the fall, so he wants to stay and take advantage of any pay increase."

"What about the tutoring?" Lynne asked, unconvinced.

"That doesn't go in the household budget." Sylvia took a breath, debating how much to reveal. Finally, she just plunged in. "That's extra money. My money. I've always wanted to travel, and, since Daddy won't retire for several more months, I decided to take some trips on my own."

"Mom, that's wonderful. Have you decided where you want to go? Will you drive or take the train or what?"

"Actually, I found a group that travels together. There are folks who are single, widowed, or divorced; but there are also married people whose spouses can't travel with them. Lila Haggerty told me about them. She's gone on several of their trips.

"I went to their meeting the other night and met some of the people. They're really friendly. And I ran into another professor from Grand Valley who retired a year ago and travels with the group, too."

"That sounds perfect. I hope you're planning to join them."

"I'm thinking about it, but I wasn't sure how you kids would feel about me traveling with a singles' group."

"I think it's wonderful. Not that you need our permission or anything. And, as for my brothers, well—" Lynne sighed and Sylvia could imagine her rolling her eyes. "Those two stud muffins are so busy playing Chi-Town's most eligible bachelors that they don't have time to think about anything more serious than what club to visit next."

Chapter Twelve

On Saturday, Dave nursed his cold beer and tended one of six barbeque grills at the Davis Andrew company picnic. He and the other managers had already cooked dozens of burgers and hot dogs and at least a small flock of chickens, but people were still arriving and the food line seemed to never get shorter. He and a handful of other volunteers continued cooking so younger team members could join their families and dine at one of the tables in the pavilion or on blankets spread on the sprawling park lawn. Grilling was hot work, especially on such a humid day, but Dave preferred holding a barbeque fork to having to make small talk.

It was different for Sylvia. She loved socializing and had a gift for making those around her feel comfortable. She didn't recognize that about herself, though. She always claimed to be an introvert. But his wife could strike up a conversation with a perfect stranger and talk about almost any subject. Dave struggled with that sort of thing. Even around friends, if conversation lagged, he had a hard time knowing what to say to fill the gap. He was much more comfortable with his nose buried in a newspaper or one of his spreadsheets than trying to act like a genial host.

Wondering how much longer he'd need to make like a grill master, he took a sip of his cold beer and managed to sneak a peek at his watch in the process. Could it really be only ten minutes since the last time he'd checked, or had his watch stopped? He shrugged and flipped a couple pieces of chicken that looked almost done. At least, manning the grill gave him something to do.

The picnic area was filled with employees and their families, eating or visiting with friends on this final long weekend of the summer. A group of energetic high school boys tossed around a plastic disk near the pond, trying to impress a group of girls, who tried to act like they hadn't noticed. It wasn't that long ago that his three would have been out there, too. He missed having them at the picnic even though they'd long outgrown the competitions put on by the planning committee. But he and the boys always enjoyed discussing sports. They'd been avid Tiger fans all their lives, cheering for their team no matter how good or bad the season had been. If living in Chicago caused them to move their allegiance to the Cubs, it would make for some pretty heated discussions when they came home for the holidays. On the other hand, Lynne had never supported any one team. For as long as he could remember, his daughter had always cheered for whatever team was the underdog in a game.

His gaze moved past the families and the teenagers to the spot near the ball diamond where Sylvia sat on a picnic blanket, watching the softball game some of the young singles had organized. In denim shorts and a white t-shirt, with her dark hair tied back with a scarf, she looked as slender and youthful as anyone on the field. Some of the players most have thought the same thing, because two of the young guys suddenly waved an invitation to Sylvia to join the game. Even though his wife laughed and shook her head, declining the invitation, Dave's jaw tensed and his fist tightened on the barbeque fork. He didn't relax again until he saw the two men turn back to the game.

A part of Dave was proud that Sylvia still had the power to turn men's heads, but a larger part of him didn't like it. He knew it was now increasingly acceptable for older women to attract younger men, but not when the woman was his wife. Those young jocks could just go and find someone else.

"Hey, guy, how ya doin'?" A cheery male voice interrupted Dave's thoughts and a beefy hand clapped him on the shoulder. He winced slightly, but pasted a smile on his face and turned to greet his vice president.

Roger Bentley was a former football player who towered several inches over Dave's own six-foot-two height. He was always friendly and outgoing, but that afternoon, he seemed a shade too loud and overly effusive.

"How you doin', Dave?" he asked again. "Are you enjoying the picnic?"

"I'm doing fine, thanks. How about you? Is your family having a good time?"

The VP shrugged, took a big sip of his can of cola then wiped his mouth with the back of his hand. Dave smelled the alcohol on the man's breath when Bentley leaned closer. "Don't know," he confided in a loud stage whisper. "They up and left me last week."

"Did they go on a trip for the long weekend?"

"No, they *left* me. Joyce took them back to Atlanta. Said she couldn't take the cold anymore. She wanted me to go with them, but how could I just up and leave?" He sipped his drink and stared morosely in the distance. "Doesn't she realize this is my job? This is what pays for our homes and cars and tuition for the girls' fancy schools."

Dave stared at his boss, at a loss for words. How was he supposed to respond to that? Should he say he was sorry or agree with his rant? He wished Sylvie were at his side. She'd know what to say.

****

Sylvia sat on her picnic blanket, pretending to watch the softball game but wishing she were almost anywhere else. Usually, she enjoyed Dave's company outings, mingling with the other couples she'd come to know over the years. She always felt so proud to be at Dave's side. You could tell by the way people behaved around him that his co-workers really liked him and respected his opinions.

Funny how Dave never saw that. If it were up to him, he'd probably skip these functions, but she always convinced him to attend. She knew Davis Andrews liked their management team to attend all the company events, so it was good for his career. But she also had a selfish motive for making him attend: she like being at his side.

However, Dave had barely been around today. For most of the picnic, he'd been with the managers and big wigs, and had pretty much ignored her. Now, watching the slimmer, younger women play softball, Sylvia remembered Anne's comment that Dave probably wondered what happened to the girl he married. She hated to admit it, but she knew she *had* changed. She'd like to believe that she could still run around like the kids out on the field, but she knew if she did, she'd pay the price for it the next day.

It took her longer to get over the aches and pains, too. Sylvia frowned. She didn't know if Dave missed the girl he'd married, but she sure did. She hadn't really let herself go, but she'd also made only a token effort to counteract the signs of aging. Was Dave ashamed of the gray in her hair and the wrinkles around her eyes? She glanced down at her hands, noticing the wrinkles there, too.

"Look out!"

Sylvia glanced up at the sudden shout to find a monstrous, white sphere racing at her. There was no time to get out of the way or even to duck before the line drive connected with her forehead. The force of the hit knocked off her sunglasses and drove her backward, flattening her to the ground.

"Are you okay? Do you need a doctor?"

Sylvia lay on the blanket and blinked her eyes against a sudden brightness that nearly blinded her. Her head hurt, too, especially with all these strangers leaning over her and talking at the same time. Who were they, and what was she doing laying here on the ground? For a minute, she panicked, unable to remember.

"Syl, honey! Are you okay?"

She recognized that voice, but why were Dave and all these other people hovering around her and looking so worried?

She closed her eyes for a moment, trying to think. After a moment, she recalled a shouted warning and a ball flying toward her face. She opened her eyes, nodded at the people around her, then winced at the sudden pain the motion caused.

"I'm okay. Really I am," she replied, scraping up a shaky smile. "I just don't think I'll be posing for any close-up photos for a while."

Chapter Thirteen

Sylvia could hardly contain her excitement as she boarded the Traveling Solo bus three weeks later. She was finally on her way to visit historic Mackinac Island.

After quickly greeting the bus driver and Deanna, their tour guide, she scooted into an empty row of seats and slid to the window so she could wave goodbye to Dave. A twinge of disappointment dampened her excitement when she looked out and saw an empty spot where he'd been parked. Apparently, her husband hadn't felt the need to stick around and see her off. Still, her enthusiasm quickly reasserted itself as more of the group entered the bus. They ranged in age from mid-twenties to late-seventies, but everyone was cordial. Even people she hadn't met at the group meetings gave her a friendly smile as they found seats. Everyone seemed as excited as she was, too.

The travel company certainly hadn't skimped on any of the amenities when they'd outfitted the bus, she thought, contrasting it to Dave's gloomy predictions.

The seats were plush and roomy with various controls built into the wide arm rests. A large button, much like the control on her van, moved her whole seat back and forth, another adjusted the angle of the backrest. There was a button to raise and lower the built-in footrest, and one that operated an overhead air vent. A compartment in the armrest flipped up to reveal a small, goose-necked reading light coiled inside. The lamp could be used at night or in gloomy weather without interfering with the driver's vision.

Her friend, Marcia, hadn't signed up for this trip—due to Eric's condition, she only made a few trips a year and always picked places she'd never been before. However, she'd encouraged Sylvia to take the excursion to the historic island, assuring her it would be everything she expected and more.

When everyone was on board, Deanna gave a slightly over–the-top welcome speech then laid out the day's itinerary. They'd make two stops on the way to Mackinaw City: one to pick up a few passengers in Mt. Pleasant, and another for lunch around noon. Finally, she settled in a seat behind the driver and the bus took off. Sylvia pulled the newest issue of Quilting World from her tote bag, intending to read for a bit, but was too excited to focus on the articles. She set the magazine on the empty seat beside her and leaned back to enjoy the scenery.

The last three weeks had been hectic ones. She'd taken on several extra students who just needed a little help catching up after their summer vacation. Most of them would be gone after a few weeks of coaching, but Sylvia enjoyed being able to tuck the additional money into her travel account. She'd also been walking every day on the new trails at the community park. Besides being good exercise, doctors said daily walks also helped to prevent osteoporosis. Retirement gave her the time to finally make the commitment to start walking.

What a surprise it had been to learn the daily walks also toned her up. She'd discovered how much just the night before when she was packing for her trip. Looking for slacks to wear, she'd come across her favorite pair of jeans shoved in the back of the closet where she'd put them months before when they'd become a little too snug to wear. On a whim, she decided to try them on. Not only did they fit, they were actually a shade loose. She was so excited she hurried down to the den to see if Dave noticed, but, sadly, he hadn't even looked up from his paper.

Determined not to let the memory ruin her excitement, Sylvia reached for her tote bag and took out an old recipe box that was held shut with a thick rubber band. Removing the band, she lifted the lid. Small one-and-a-half-inch squares of fabric filled the container. Stripes, plaids, ginghams, and florals. Each square was in some shade of cranberry, mauve, or burgundy. The tiny squares would be used to make a six-inch quilt block, following the Calico Heart pattern Sylvia loved.

Originally, she'd planned to make one block for every place she and Dave visited together. His refusal to travel with her had temporarily derailed the plans. But no more. She would still make the travel quilt, even if she had to do her traveling by herself. As the bus sped north, Sylvia had fun flipping through the colorful squares, picking out her favorites, and trying various combinations to make the first block of this special quilt. With her hands occupied, the miles passed quickly.

Four women and two men joined the group in Mt. Pleasant. Sylvia was prepared to put away her quilt supplies to make room for the newcomers, but there were plenty of other empty seats. Once the bus headed out again, she continued to hand sew the various squares together to form a heart.

Shortly before noon, the bus stopped at a small café near Gaylord. A handful of dusty pickup trucks and older cars were in the lot; a shiny, black Mercedes parked near the restaurant door. A muscular blond in a dark shirt and pants leaned casually against the driver's door with his muscular arms crossed over his broad chest.

Fluffing out her hair, Deanna leaned toward the women sitting across from her and winked. "I sure wouldn't mind getting me some of *that*!"

The tour leader made a show of descending from the bus first and calling back instructions to their driver in a sultry voice designed to be heard across the lot. However, her little performance seemed to miss its mark. The driver of the luxury car didn't even glance in her direction. Sylvia smothered a chuckle as the group leader called a few additional instructions to the group members with the same result. Finally, with a derisive sniff and a toss of her long brown curls, the young woman stalked into the restaurant, leaving the others to follow her.

Sylvia fished a pair of sunglasses from her purse and put them on before leaving the bus. The September day was nice and sunny, but the temperature was a good deal colder than it had been in Grand Rapids. It was bound to be even cooler at night on the island. As she crossed the lot to the restaurant door, she went over the list of things she'd packed and wondered if the clothes would be warm enough. Busy with her thoughts, she ran right into a tall, dark-haired man, who was exiting the café just as she reached for the door. Juggling his phone and a take-out bag, the stranger reached out a hand to steady her. "*Pardonnez-moi.*"

"Not at all. It was my fault," Sylvia apologized. "I was worried about the weather and wasn't paying attention."

"But the weather is lovely, is eet not?" he asked. His eyes were hidden behind a pair of dark, wraparound sunglasses, but his smile was nearly as charming as his French accent.

"It is now, but it is bound to be much colder when we get to the island."

"We?" He looked past her to the parking lot then nodded when he saw the big tour bus. He gave her hand a little squeeze and smiled again. "Traveling Solo?" he read. "You are with the group, *non*?"

"I am with the group, yes." She laughed and freed her hand from his grasp. "And if I don't get inside and order, they'll be leaving without me."

"I am sure they would not be so heartless as to abandon such a lovely female."

Sylvia laughed again, amused at the handsome stranger's charm. "Nonetheless, I don't want to keep them waiting. If you'll excuse me?"

"But, of course," he said, bowing slightly as he opened the door for her. "Have a most pleasant lunch."

Sylvia thanked him then scooted into the café. Most of the others were already seated at small tables for four or six. She glanced around, looking for an empty chair, and spotted Deanna motioning to a spot at her table.

"*Who* is that?" the group leader asked as soon as Sylvia was seated.

Sylvia turned her head to see who the woman was pointing to and saw the man she'd bumped into standing by the tour bus, talking to their driver. She shrugged and turned back to study the menu. "We bumped into one another in the doorway and exchanged apologies, but that was it."

"You should have gotten his number."

"Deanna." Sylvia chuckled. "If I got the number of every person I've bumped into, I'd have a book as thick as the New York City phone directory."

The younger woman didn't seem to agree, but the waitress arrived at their table, so they dropped the subject and ordered.

Chapter Fourteen

Mackinac Bridge.

Sylvia could hardly believe her eyes when they reached Mackinaw City and she got her first glimpse of the bridge. The five-mile-long structure connecting Michigan's upper and lower peninsulas was the longest suspension bridge in the entire Western Hemisphere. It contained more than forty-two thousand miles of cables that sparkled in the sunlight.

Photos simply couldn't do justice to the mammoth structure. She wished Dave was there to see it, too. It would be incredible to drive over the bridge to St. Ignace and catch a ferry to the island from there. However, they'd save tolls by boarding on this side of the strait.

She gathered up her belongings when they reached the ferry dock, where they'd board a three-story catamaran for a fifteen-minute trip to the island. While their bus driver transferred their luggage to a flat cart, she and the others followed Deanna inside, where she purchased their tickets.

As soon as she had her ticket, Sylvia hurried over to the terminal windows, where she could watch the seamen move luggage and cargo on board and prepare for the next leg of her trip. Around her, the other group members chatted happily and appeared to take all the hustle and bustle for granted. None of them seemed quite as excited or awed by the sights and sounds of the busy ferry dock. Maybe, they were so used to traveling they weren't impressed by the sight of the picturesque lakefront town or the symphony of calling seagulls and ringing ship bells. But for Sylvia, everything she saw and experienced was an exciting first.

When things were ready, she boarded the ferry with the others and followed Deanna to a huge enclosed sitting area on the second-level deck. Large windows gave a nice view of the scenery, but Sylvia would have liked to go topside to sit. Unfortunately, despite the sunshine, there was already a biting wind coming off the water, and it would be intensified by the boat's speed once they took off. Since her jacket was in her luggage, Sylvia knew she'd get too cold to enjoy the ride. Instead, she settled for a seat by the window where she'd be able to get some good pictures.

No one else appeared interested in taking photos. In fact, most of her traveling companions headed for inside seats, well away from the windows. The sound of their happy conversation mingled pleasantly with the thrum of the ferry's engines. For a moment, Sylvia wished she had someone to chat with and share the excitement. If Dave hadn't been so silly, they could have been enjoying the boat ride together on this beautiful fall day.

But here she was all alone. Just her and her digital camera. She refused to waste this breathtaking scenery by engaging in a pity party. Although no one was there to share the experience now, she would take some photos to share with her friends later. She turned to face the window and leaned her hip against one of the seat backs to brace herself, snapping pictures of the dock and shoreline. A ferry from a different transit line passed by, and Sylvia took a couple pictures of it, too. That was the beauty of a digital camera. She could snap shots all day then sort through them later and simply delete the lousy ones.

Sylvia caught a whiff of pleasant, spicy cologne a split-second before a deep baritone spoke behind her. "Is this seat taken?"

Startled, she nearly dropped her camera as she spun around to stare into the most gorgeous eyes she'd ever seen. Smoky gray and fringed with long, sooty black lashes.

"Women would kill for lashes like those."

Oh my! Had she really just said that out loud?

Cheeks blazing, she quickly averted her gaze away and busied herself gathering up her purse and tote bag. "No. Nobody is sitting here. Just me. Oh my! Let me gather up this mess."

Good grief! Now I'm babbling like an idiot. The guy is going to think I'm certifiable.

She snuck a peek at the stranger beneath her lashes and was relieved to find him smiling. Suddenly, recognition hit her. "You're the man from the restaurant. What are you doing here?"

"I am part of the bus tour. Traveling Solo, *non*?"

"No. I mean, yes. I mean, you weren't on the bus earlier."

"I was not," he agreed. "I talked to your driver and joined the tour here."

"But why?"

He gave a shrug. "I am here on the business. But have been, how do you say eet, touring the sights? I heard about this island and wished to visit."

"Me, too," Sylvia admitted. "I've read so much about it, but never got a chance to visit it before."

"*Tres bien.* We can tour eet together, *non*?" He held out his hand and smiled. "I am Etienne Dumas."

"And I'm Sylvia...Sylvia Miller."

As they sat down and started to chat about the island's history, Sylvia briefly wondered how Dave would react if he saw her not only talking to a strange man, but also agreeing to tour the island with him. It was perfectly harmless. They were on a tour, and the man merely wanted company for sightseeing. Surely, Dave couldn't object to that.

At least, she hoped not.

By the time the ferry landed, Sylvia had learned Etienne was from Quebec and a recent widower. He hadn't really dwelled on that except to explain he'd started traveling more frequently for his company since his wife's death as it kept him busy. Etienne had kept up a flow of entertaining conversation, and Sylvia hadn't had to do much more than smile and nod. At one point, she'd glanced over at the rest of the group and saw Deanna watching them. She didn't know if she should be flattered or embarrassed when the tour director had winked and given her a thumbs-up sign. Surely, Deanna didn't think the man meant anything by his attention. He was just lonely, and—good grief—she was a married woman.

Still, the attention was nice. It was rather like the day in high school when the star quarterback had sat down next to her in the student center. They both knew he'd only sat down to wait for his girlfriend, the school's popular homecoming queen, to finish with her cheer practice. But Sylvia had enjoyed talking to him anyway. They'd laughed about a funny incident in class and discussed an upcoming assignment. She knew nothing would come of their encounter, but for a little while, it had made her feel special.

She felt the same way talking to Etienne.

When they reached the island, Deanna herded everyone to the "taxicab" stand. Since vehicles weren't permitted on the island, a line of colorful horse-drawn carriages, with drivers in top hats and full livery, waited to take them to the Grand Hotel. Their luggage would follow later in a draft cart.

Etienne took Sylvia's hand and led her to the lead carriage. Before she realized what he was about, he put his hands on her waist and swung her up to the middle seat.

However, she could hardly protest his actions since he turned and lifted several other women into the vehicle, too, before finally taking a seat beside her.

The ride to the beautiful hotel, where the movie *Somewhere in Time* had been filmed, was a wonderful mini-tour in itself. Their driver took them past old Fort Mackinac, beautiful Arch Rock, and to a spot where they could see the replica of the Statue of Liberty that had been donated to the island by the Boy Scouts of America. When they finally arrived at the main entrance, footmen helped them from their horse-drawn taxies and directed them to the reception desk to check in.

The minute she walked through the doorway, Sylvia felt like she'd been transported into another era. The 125-year-old hotel offered guests a taste of how the wealthy had lived during Victorian times. Everywhere she looked, her eyes feasted on beautiful antiques and artwork. The hotel had 385 rooms with no two being alike. Sylvia had opted for one of the less expensive, interior rooms when she'd signed up for the tour, but her accommodations were nothing short of sumptuous, from the thick pile carpeting to the luxurious furnishings. But there was too much to do to waste any more time indoors. She quickly freshened her make-up, changed into a warm sweatshirt, then hurried down to rejoin the others.

The group had no formal agenda on the island. Everyone was free to explore, shop, or just relax on the hotel's famous front porch. Deanna gave each of them an information packet about the island and said they could choose between walking, bicycling, or riding in a carriage to get around the island. Then they were on their own until dinner in the Main Dining Room that evening. A few in the group headed into the hotel's various gift shops, but Etienne, Sylvia, and most of the others rode a horse-drawn taxi to the picturesque town down the hill from the hotel.

"So," Etienne asked as the cart bumped its way down the cobbled street, the horses' hooves clopping against the road. "Do you prefer to shop? Or to see the island?"

"Of course, I want to shop for souvenirs. I couldn't possibly go home without buying some fudge. However, I'm more interested in seeing the island first. But I have to warn you. I'm not much of a cyclist. The walking tour appeals to me a lot more."

"I rode a bicycle in my younger days, but now, I too prefer to—how do you say eet—take eet the easy way?" The way he spoke reminded Sylvia of the charming black-and-white movies her mother used to watch in the afternoons. Back then she'd thought the suave men with the foreign accents were pretty hokey, but now, she could appreciate their continental charm.

The afternoon sped by as they walked around the charming island, visiting Fort Mackinac, the Mission Church, and the Indian Dormitory museum. They even caught a boat over to nearby Round Island to visit the famous lighthouse there. Sylvia took so many pictures she thought she'd never remember half of what they were. Etienne insisted on taking her picture by the Fort Mackinac sign and in front of several of the sites they visited so she'd have them for souvenirs. At the end of the day, they hurried into one of the fudge shops and bought several varieties of the confection.

Etienne hired a two-person carriage to drive them directly back to the Grand Hotel as the sun began to set. Sylvia enjoyed seeing the lights of the hotel crowning the hill as they approached the entrance.

"This has been a wonderful day," she enthused then smothered a yawn.

Etienne laughed. "Do not fall asleep yet. You do not want to miss dinner in the Main Dining Room at seven. I hear the desserts are *magnifique*."

Sylvia glanced at her watch. "Then I'd better hurry so I

won't be late."

Chapter Fifteen

"Ah there you are. How beautiful you look, *cherie.*"

Sylvia was glad she'd taken the time to put on make-up and curl her hair when she saw Etienne waiting for her in the foyer. His beautifully cut suit made her feel slightly underdressed in her simple black knit dress. But he bent over her hand with continental flair and flattered her profusely as he escorted her into the Grand Hotel's Main Dining Room.

She was surprised and a bit uncomfortable when Etienne slipped the maître d' a sizable tip and asked for a table away from the others. Before she could protest, they were seated in comfortable green-and-white striped satin chairs across the room, and Etienne had ordered a superb local wine for them. While the wine steward went to get the bottle, they rehashed the day's adventure. A moment later, a slight commotion at the dining room entrance caught their attention as well as that of the other diners.

"Hello there!" Deanna called from the doorway, waving to get their attention. "Hello."

The tour leader headed across the elegant dining room directly toward their table, ignoring the protests of the maître d' who followed in her wake. A strapless leather mini-dress that was barely wider than some of Sylvia's belts hugged the young woman's generous curves, and strappy stiletto heels accented her shapely legs.

"Etienne," she said, resting her hand on his shoulder, "would you please tell this poor man that it's okay for me to join the two of you?" She turned toward Sylvia and smiled. "It *is* okay for me to join you, isn't it?"

"But, of course," Etienne replied, rising to his feet and giving her a courtly bow. He motioned to the waiter, who brought another chair and table setting for her. "What would you like to drink, my dear?"

As he leaned closer to Deanna to discuss her drink options, Sylvia couldn't help but feel like the homecoming queen had just reclaimed the high school quarterback. Irritated with herself for feeling that way, she forced herself to relax and enjoy the wonderful five-course meal. The three of them lingered over dessert and their after dinner drinks, laughing and talking. Suddenly, Sylvia glanced at her watch. *How could it possibly have gotten so late?*

"Would you two please excuse me?" she asked, standing up and putting her napkin on her plate. "I just noticed the time, and I still have a phone call I need to make."

As soon as she was out of sight of the dining room door, Sylvia bent to remove her high heels so she could hurry faster to her room. It was nearly midnight and she should have called Dave hours ago. How could she have so totally lost track of time? She nearly ran through the halls, grateful the thick carpeting muffled the sound of her footsteps. Juggling her shawl and purse, she paused at her room and fumbled for her door key.

"Allow me, *s'il vous plait.*"

Startled by Etienne's unexpected appearance, Sylvia jerked and her purse slipped from her grasp. Lipstick, cell phone, hotel key, everything dumped as her purse tumbled to the ground.

Etienne's long arm shot out, and he quickly scooped up her fallen belongings. At the exact moment he rose upward to give them to her, she bent down to retrieve them.

Crack!

****

"*Cherie*, are you all right?"

Sylvia blinked open her eyes. Where was she? Why was everything so blurry? And why was there a two-headed man bending over her and babbling at her in a lovely accent?

A two-headed man?

She must really be losing it. She blinked her eyes again, and some of the fog cleared. The shape still hovered over her, but now it had only one head. A very handsome one with long, dark hair and the most amazing gray eyes. She heard him speak again, but couldn't decipher the smooth, silky words coming from his mouth.

Concentrate. Maybe if she tried harder, she'd be able to make some sense of what he was saying.

"Perhaps I should summon a doctor."

"Doctor? Is someone hurt?"

She sat up quickly then fell backward again as dizziness overcame her. She closed her eyes and felt herself lifted, floating upward and then landing on a cloud, a nice, soft, silk-covered cloud. It felt lovely to lay in the darkness and just float on the lovely softness. A cool cloth touched her forehead then settled on it. The baritone voice continued to rumble softly, murmuring to her with a French accent.

French? Yes, that was it. Now, if she could just make out the words.

After a moment that might have been either a minute or an hour, she blinked open her eyes again. This time, they focused a little better. She smiled at Etienne, sitting beside her on the bed holding a cloth to her forehead.

"You look much nicer with only one head," she commented.

He arched his brow, a confused look on his face. "One head?"

Sylvia waved a hand dismissively. "Never mind. It's nothing. I'm still a bit dazed, I think. What happened?"

"You dropped your purse, *cherie,* and everything fell out. I am so sorry. I hit your beautiful face with my head when I retrieved your keys—"

"Don't apologize. It's not your fault. It's me. I'm accident prone."

She tried again to sit up, but he pushed her back with a firm but gentle hand.

"Please do not rise. Let me ring the concierge. The hotel must have *le docteur* on call."

"Doctor? No, no. I don't need a doctor, Etienne. I'm fine, really."

"But, *cherie,* you were—how do you say eet?—knocked up?"

"Knocked *out,*" Sylvia corrected. She smiled and explained about getting knocked out by a softball just a few weekends earlier. "I'm sure that's why our little head butt did me in tonight. I'll call my own doctor as soon as I get back home and have it checked out."

"Very good. But I would feel much better if you put ice on eet."

"Fine. I can do that," she said, struggling to get up again. "I'll just get some ice and—"

"*Non,* you must rest!" Etienne insisted, pressing his hand against her shoulder to prevent her from sitting up. "I will get the ice for you. Yes?"

She nodded and closed her eyes. It really did feel much nicer to just stretch out on the bed with her eyes closed.

****

Etienne stepped into the hallway, ice bucket in hand, and quietly closed Sylvia's door, As he turned to head down the hall for ice, he spotted a small blue rectangle laying against the molding a few feet away. Sylvia's cell phone! It must have gone flying when she'd dumped her purse. He'd been so worried about getting her inside he hadn't even noticed the cell phone when he'd picked her up to carry her into her room.

He smiled, remembering how light she'd felt in his arms when he'd lifted her. She was nearly as light as his wife Elise had been on their wedding day. He'd known a lot of women since then, beautiful women he'd wooed then discarded, but this one intrigued him. From the moment he'd laid eyes on Sylvia in that quaint café this morning, he'd known he wanted to get to know her better. He'd made a quick deal with the bus driver for Sylvia's tour group—money spoke a universal language—then he'd instructed Henri to drive back to Mackinac City and drop him off at the ferry dock. His chauffeur had been completely perplexed but knew better than to question his boss's instructions.

It had been a wonderful day touring the island with the lovely American and he had planned to spend more time with her this evening. A nice dinner, some drinks, a little walk along the beach. Unfortunately, their little accident had disrupted his plans. But he wasn't about to let it end this way. He needed to stay in touch with her. He'd be back in Michigan in a few weeks. Maybe they could pick up where they'd left off.

Quickly, he retrieved the cell phone from the floor then checked it for damage. The display lit up and the touchscreen looked fine. He slid the control bar to unlock the phone, relieved when he saw Sylvia hadn't password-protected the device. With a smile, he tapped in a few digits then waited until he felt the vibration of the smart phone in his suit jacket's inside pocket. He slid out his phone and checked the readout for recent calls: *Sylvia Miller*. Below her name appeared a phone number with a 616 area code. Smiling, Etienne saved the data to his phone's contacts, pocketed it, then went off in search of ice.

Chapter Sixteen

"Welcome home!" Dave called. He swung his wife from the step of the burgundy tour bus and tipped her face toward his for a kiss.

"What in the Sam Hill?"

In the pool of light thrown by the bus's headlights, he studied Sylvia's face. An ugly purplish bruise covered most of her left cheek, and the swelling from it had puffed her eye almost shut. She grimaced and looked away, making him regret his loud outburst.

This certainly wasn't the warm welcome he'd planned as he'd driven to the high school to meet her bus. He had a nice dinner in the oven and bottle of wine cooling in the refrigerator. But seeing her bruises had driven those plans from his head. He tried again in a carefully controlled tone.

"Syl, honey, what happened to your face?"

His wife smiled ruefully. "I know this will come as a big shock to you, but your wife is a klutz."

Dave frowned at the flippant answer, started to reply, but snapped his jaw shut instead. *Here I am, trying hard to be understanding, and she's putting me off with lame jokes.*

As if reading his mind, she put her hand on his arm and led him a distance away from the others. "Look, honey, it's a long story."

"So give me the Readers' Digest condensed version."

"It was an accident. Simple as that. My head was going down, and his was going up." She gestured to her eye. "And they met in the middle."

"Some guy hit you?"

"It's not as bad as it sounds. I'll tell you all about it on the way home."

"Fine" he muttered, thrusting his hands in his jeans pockets to stem his irritation. He didn't realize he was jingling his car keys until he saw her wince again. He quickly stopped and mumbled an apology, but she seemed more interested in the luggage being unloaded than in him. No, this definitely wasn't the happy homecoming he'd envisioned.

"Where did you park?" she asked.

He waved toward the entrance. He'd been surprised to see the school all lit up and the lot nearly full when he'd arrived. "I had to park way out by the entrance. Apparently, the school must be holding some sort of function tonight."

"No. It's evening services. Covenant Ministries rents the building on Sundays."

"That explains all the cars," he said, nodding as if he'd known and just forgotten briefly, but the truth was he hadn't had a clue. Sylvia had always been the one to keep track of things like that.

One of the bus passengers called goodbye to Sylvia. She returned the greeting then glanced at those still waiting for luggage. Dave followed her gaze, suddenly noticing what a diverse group the travelers were. Surprisingly, only a handful of them were what he considered *seniors*. The rest looked to be anywhere from mid-twenties upward. Several of them, including one stunning brunette, wore t-shirts emblazoned with the group's name. Although women made up the majority, a few men waited for luggage, too. One of them looked over and waved. Dave shot a glance at Sylvia and saw her hand lift in acknowledgement.

"Who's that?" he asked, striving for a nonchalant tone.

"Etienne. He's one of the group..." She hesitated then continued. "He's the person I ran into."

Dave frowned and sized up the stranger. Tall and lean with a headful of dark, wavy hair. He judged the man to be late forties, early fifties tops. He had the build of someone who played racquetball every day to stay in shape. More the type to ride in a limo than a bus.

"It looks like they're almost done unloading," Sylvia said, pointing toward the bus. "Why don't you get the car, and I'll go get my suitcase."

"I'll come with you," he said. "You shouldn't be lifting things with a head injury."

She shrugged as if she didn't care one way or the other. But he did. He planned to make sure no other accidents happened to her. While he retrieved her overnight case, she went to say goodbye to the people mingling nearby. Dave's jaw tensed when he saw her turn toward the guy who'd given her the shiner. He hoisted the bag in one hand and hurried over to join them.

"Eet was a wonderful trip. *Tres magnifique.*"

"I enjoyed it, too. It was—"

"Are you ready?" Dave interrupted. He held out his free hand. "Hi. I'm Dave Miller, Sylvia's husband."

"Etienne Dumas," the man replied. He cordially returned Dave's handshake. "You are a lucky man. Sylvia is..." He paused and gave her a disturbingly intimate smile. "...a most charming companion."

Dave didn't care for the man's tone or the smoldering looks he gave Sylvia. Clamping his teeth together, he managed to hang on to his temper as he took her by the arm. "We should be going."

"And here is my driver as well," the other man replied as a glossy black Escalade drove up and parked a few feet away. "Eet has been a pleasure, Sylvia. 'opefully, we can do eet again."

Dave had had enough of the phony Frenchman. "The car's over this way," he said, leading her away before she could reply.

He expected her to chide him for being rude, but he didn't care. The man was too smooth in Dave's opinion. Surprisingly, Sylvia didn't say anything as they walked to the car.

Once they were buckled in, she leaned back against the headrest and closed her eyes. From the look of those bruises, she probably had quite a headache. "Did you get that checked out by a doctor?"

She shook her head, wincing slightly as she did. "It wasn't necessary. It's just a little bruise."

"I think you should have it checked. It's only a few weeks since you got knocked out on Labor Day."

"Like I said, I'm a klutz." She sighed. "But if it will make you feel better, I'll call the doctor in the morning."

"Good."

They rode in silence, lost in their own thoughts. He'd thought maybe she'd fallen asleep, but suddenly she chuckled.

"It really was just a stupid accident, Dave. I dropped my key, and Etienne picked it up just as I bent down to get it. My head was going down, his was going up, and we collided. That's all."

It sounded simple enough, but something bothered him; it nagged at the back of his mind. He debated whether to ask his question or just let the subject drop. Finally, he couldn't hold it in any longer.

"Where did you drop your keys, Syl?"

"Where? They dropped on the floor."

"No, I meant where were *you* when you dropped your

keys?"

"Oh. Outside my hotel room door."

He nearly swerved into the opposite lane at her words. "What in Sam Hill was that phony Frenchman doing outside your hotel room?"

****

"I swear, Dave, I've never seen anything quite so breathtaking in my life," Sylvia exclaimed as she poured their morning coffee. "The climb to the top of the lighthouse had me panting, but the view was really worth it."

Dave listened with half an ear, but he couldn't have repeated anything she told him. All he could think was how young and radiant she looked even with her swollen eye and bruised cheek. She nearly bubbled over with joy and excitement, just as she had in their younger days whenever she had talked about her dreams and the places she wanted to see. Sylvia was so beautiful. Back then, he would have done anything for her, promised her anything just to see that wonderful smile.

Back then? He frowned. Why did that sound so selfish? What about *now?*

These days, he was more cautious, more responsible. There were things he could no longer do. He got tired more easily and ran out of energy quicker.

Good grief. He sounded like an old man. Well, he was an old man, nearer to sixty than fifty. He'd never really cared about age before, but suddenly, it seemed like the years had snuck up on him.

He looked over at his wife. Sylvia was older, too. A few lines bracketed her mouth and crinkled around her eyes. But she had the same shiny black hair, the same determination to her step. Age didn't seem to have affected her. She stayed in great shape. In fact, he thought as she bent to retrieve a pan of biscuits from the oven, she looked better in jeans now than she had back in college.

"Earth to Dave. Earth to Dave. Are you there?"

He blinked. "What?"

"It's almost seven-thirty. Are you going to work today, or did you take the day off?"

"Work. Right. I need to get going. I have a big meeting with Rog this morning. Can't be late."

"No, of course you can't."

Was it his imagination or did Sylvia suddenly seem subdued, less bubbly? Was her eye bothering her? She'd assured him it was nothing the night before, but it probably hurt more than she'd wanted to let on. He swallowed down the last of his coffee then gave her a quick peck on her good cheek.

"Don't forget to get that eye checked," he reminded her as he rushed out the door.

Chapter Seventeen

"Hello, welcome back! We missed you last week." Anne rushed over to greet Sylvia as soon as she arrived at The Stitching Post for the Tuesday night meeting. "We're all eager to hear—"

The shop clerk suddenly froze, her eyes widening as she spotted the huge bruise discoloring Sylvia's face, despite her carefully applied make-up. Anne glanced furtively around the shop then took her friend by the arm and drew her aside.

"What happened to your eye?" she whispered.

"This?" Sylvia touched her left cheek and wrinkled her nose distastefully. "Would you believe I knocked heads with another traveler on my bus trip? It was a real mess last week, all black and blue and swollen. That's why I wasn't here last Tuesday."

Seeing the younger woman's concern, she smiled reassuringly. "I'm a lot better this week. Honest."

"Didn't you just have another bad bruise a few weeks ago?"

Sylvia nodded. "I stopped a softball the hard way at Dave's company picnic. I seem to be really accident-prone lately."

Anne studied her for a moment then took a deep breath. "I understand about *accidents*, Sylvia. Believe me, I really understand," she confided. "And I'm here if you ever want to talk to someone. Just call me, okay?"

Puzzled by the intensity of her young friend's tone, Sylvia frowned. She wasn't quite sure how to answer, so she merely nodded her head. It seemed sufficient. Anne gave her arm another pat then hurried away to help one of the other quilters. Sylvia watched her for a long moment before shouldering her project bag and going toward the back of the shop to join her friends.

"Whoa! What happened to your eye?" Lila asked in response to Sylvia's greeting.

"That seems to be a popular question tonight. Anne just asked me the same thing."

"Well, it's pretty hard to overlook, honey. Even if you did a pretty good job covering it with your foundation."

"Obviously, not well enough."

"So what happened to you?"

"I had a run in—literally—with one of the other travelers on my bus trip. He zigged. I zagged. *Et Voila!*"

"He?" Tee asked, joining them in time to hear Sylvia's explanation. She dropped her tote bag on the chair opposite Lila's and carefully removed her suit jacket.

"Yep. A handsome Canadian businessman from Quebec."

"*Ooo la la!* Does Dave know?"

"There is nothing to *know*. Etienne merely stooped down to get the keys I'd dropped at the same time I went for them. Our heads collided."

"Dropped keys? Is that today's version for the old dropped handkerchief?" Lila asked, her eyes twinkling mischievously.

"Oh, stop it you two. Etienne was just a fellow traveler." Sylvia paused as Anne joined the group to see if anyone wanted coffee or tea. "You know, Anne, I should drag you along on my next trip. Etienne is a few years older than you, but he's ever so sexy with that French accent of his."

"Oh no!" Anne held up her hands as if to ward off the suggestion. "I don't care how sexy this Etienne person might be. I am definitely not interested."

"Why not?" Lila asked, her interest obviously piqued by the young clerk's vehemence.

"Maybe Anne already has a hot young boyfriend," Tee suggested.

"I don't have one, and I don't want one," the clerk responded then hurried away to get beverages.

"Who has a hot new boyfriend?" Ellen said by way of greeting as she, Sue, and Doris arrived together. "Holy cow, Sylvia! Who'd you get in a fight with?"

"Very funny, Ellie May," Sylvia responded, using the nickname her best friend detested. "You know very well what happened. I told you all about it when we had coffee last week."

"I know, but I love to tease you. Although, I must say, ladies, she looks a lot better today than she did when I saw her."

"One can hope," Sylvia murmured. She took the mug of tea Anne offered her and cupped her hands around it. "Thanks, Anne. This feels so good tonight. I can't believe how cold it turned."

"It's supposed to get colder. The guys are hoping there'll be snow for opening day," Sue told them, referring to Michigan's deer hunting season that would start mid-month. Her husband Frank and his brothers, all farmers in nearby Walker, looked forward to this time of year when the crops were in and they had a bit more leisure time.

"I never understood the attraction of sitting in the woods outdoors in the winter," Ellen remarked, pulling her quilt from her project bag. "I prefer looking at snow through my front window."

As the rest of the group arrived, Sylvia received more good-natured ribbing about her eye. However, everyone soon settled down to work on their various projects. Most of the women were making gift items for the holidays, but a few had baby quilts or other items to sew.

"How's your quilt coming, Lila?" Sylvia asked as the older woman carefully outlined a colorful snowman with parallel rows of tiny stitches.

"Pretty good. I've got most of the snowmen echo quilted," she said, holding up the piece so Sylvia could see the tiny rows of precise stitches outlining the shape of each character. "By the end of the week, I'll be ready to chalk mark the quilting design and start it. What are you working on tonight? You finished the baby quilt for Lynne's friend, didn't you?"

"Almost. It's taken longer than I expected. I've been doing a lot of extra tutoring."

Lila nodded. "Putting aside money for your next trip? Are you going on the one the girls were telling me about?"

"You mean the one to Branson?" Sylvia asked then continued when Lila nodded. "I don't think so. Deanna called me about it, but seven days is an awfully long time to be gone this time of the year," Sylvia said, carefully basting a small sailboat on a square of bright yellow fabric. "Thanksgiving is only a few weeks away, and I haven't even begun my Christmas shopping yet."

"I figured this might not be a good time for you, but Marcia heard about your mishap and wanted to make sure it hadn't soured you on the group."

"Hardly! I can't blame anyone but myself for what happened." Sylvia chuckled. "What about you? Are you going to make the trip?"

Lila held up the snowman quilt. "Not if I want to get this quilt and Pastor Steve's gift done in time for Christmas. But it does sound like it would have been fun."

"Why not use the new quilter?" Sylvia suggested, pointing to the area where Myra assisted another member of the group with the long-arm sewing machine. "You could have it stitched in a couple hours instead of a couple weeks."

"I know, but it just wouldn't feel right to me. I've always hand-stitched the gifts I give to people. I'll go another time. There will be plenty of other trips."

Sylvia nodded and threaded her needle with bright blue floss to whip stitch the edges of the boat's sail. After knotting the floss, she drew the needle carefully through the fabric. Concentrating on keeping her stitches even, she tuned out the sound of the machine humming in the corner as well as the snippets of conversation going on around her.

"Isn't that sad news about Katie?" Ellen asked, sitting down beside her.

Sylvia looked up and glanced around the store. She hadn't noticed the quiet receptionist wasn't with their group that evening. "Where is she? Did something happen?"

Ellen nodded. "You know how eager she's been to quit her job as soon as their credit cards were paid off?"

She nodded. "Yes. Last time we talked, she told me she hoped to be able to quit after the holidays since they've been putting her entire paycheck toward paying down the balances."

"That's what she thought," Ellen said. "Then, yesterday, the credit card bill came in the mail, and she decided to check the balance. She was shocked to see the card was almost maxed out."

Sylvia gasped. "That's awful! But why didn't she know about it sooner?"

"Phil always paid the bills," Ellen explained. "So she never really looked at them. She left it all to him. Last night, she called me all upset at the discovery."

For as long as Sylvia had known Ellen, her friend had

always been the person others turned to when they needed a sounding board or a shoulder to lean on. It was no surprise to hear Katie had turned to Ellen, too. "What did Phil say?"

"She hasn't been able to ask him. He's gone on one of his business trips again, and Katie doesn't want to talk to him about it over the phone. She says she wants to be able to look him in the eye when she confronts him with the bill."

"I can understand that," Sylvia said, grateful that Dave was so dependable. She picked up her quilt block, intending to continue the applique work, when a sudden thought struck her. Would she know if Dave suddenly blew through their saving and ran them into debt? He paid all their bills, too. But he'd changed so much recently. Could their finances be the reason for his late nights and this sudden reluctance to retire and travel with her?

Just that evening, he'd asked if she was making any more travel plans. At the time, Sylvia thought maybe he'd changed his mind about traveling, so she told him about a four-day shopping excursion Traveling Solo had planned. The trip would take them to Gurnee Mills and Chicago then head for the famous Christmas shop in Frankenmuth, Michigan. Instead of wanting to come along, Dave had dragged out the same one-note symphony about not needing to spend money to go on a trip just to buy stuff he didn't need. Or at least that's how it had sounded before she'd tuned him out.

Now, after hearing about Katie and Phil's financial problems, Sylvia wondered if Dave's resistance masked some deeper issue. Could a financial disaster lurk around the corner for her, too? Could that be why he worked more hours than ever lately, and why he shut her out whenever she brought up his retirement? Things couldn't go on this way. Something had to give. Sylvia just hoped it wouldn't be their marriage.

Chapter Eighteen

"Hello?"

"Sylvia, *comment-allez vous?*"

"Etienne?" Sylvia asked, surprised to hear his velvety smooth voice coming from her cell phone. "I—I'm fine. How are you?"

"Very lonely without you, *cherie.*"

She blinked, uncertain how to take his remark. Was it just continental charm or was the man actually flirting with her? Before she could decide, he continued.

"When will you be making another trip?"

"I'm not sure," Sylvia hedged. "Exams are coming up, then the holidays, and several of the students I tutor now need extra help with their studies. Why do you ask?"

"Deanna from the tour group called. There is a trip to Chicago next weekend. Shopping then a play at one of the dinner theaters. I would be very happy if you would go."

Sylvia glanced at the calendar beside the breakfast bar and checked the date. Although it was the weekend before Christmas, amazingly, they had nothing planned.

"That might be fun. Our two sons live in Chicago, but I've

never been to the city. I hear it's beautiful during the holidays. I wonder if my husband can—"

"If he cannot, we can keep each other company, *non*. After all, that is what Traveling Solo is about, *n'est pas?*"

She wasn't sure how to respond to that, so she merely mumbled something non-committal.

Etienne didn't seem to notice her non-reply. "The coordinator, Deana, she also told me of another trip. Eet is after the holidays to Traverse City for a concert by The Londoners. Do you know of this group?"

"The Londoners? Oh my goodness. Of course I know of them. They were very popular when Dave and I were in college. Not as big as the Beatles, but they had some really good songs."

He rattled off a few more particulars then warned her that Deanna had told him registrations were filling up fast for this outing.

"That's understandable. It's extremely rare for them to perform in the Midwest. The concert is sure to be sold out."

"So you will go?" he asked. When she didn't reply right away, he tried again. "Promise me you will at least think about eet, *cherie*."

"I will, I promise. It sounds very tempting, but the tickets are probably pretty expensive. I'll have to discuss it with Dave before I decide."

"But of course. Still, I think you are, as they say, a woman who owns her mind, *non*?"

Sylvia smiled at the Gallic twist he gave the idiom. "Yes, Etienne. I do have a mind of my own, but I like to share things with David. I enjoy doing things together with him. That's why I married him."

"*Mais oui*, that is as eet should be," he hurried to agree. "Your David is a most fortunate man."

"That's charming of you to say, but I'm sure there are times when he wouldn't agree with you."

"How could he not?" Etienne asked just as the phone line started to crackle. *"Merde!* I am losing the signal. I will talk to you in a few days, *cherie."*

"Okay. Talk to you later."

She disconnected the phone then turned to the built-in oven to check the progress of dinner. The glass of the oven door reflected someone standing behind her. Startled, she spun around to find Dave leaning in the kitchen doorway.

"Hi, honey. I didn't hear you come in."

"Obviously. Who. Is. Etienne?"

Surprised by Dave's tone, it took her a few moments to register his words. Pretending not to notice the anger, she gave a dismissive wave then turned back the oven. "Etienne Dumas. You met him when you picked me up from my trip. He's one of the Traveling Solo group members. Remember?"

"The klutz who gave you the black eye?"

"Well, I'd hardly describe Etienne as a klutz." She chuckled, thinking of the smoothly elegant Canadian. "But yes, he's the one I bumped heads with."

Dave muttered something then turned and headed down the hallway.

"Honey, dinner's almost ready," Sylvia called after him. "I made your favorite. Meatloaf and baked potatoes."

"Eat without me," he replied without breaking his stride. "I'm not hungry."

Chapter Nineteen

"Sylvia, I'm home," Dave called then frowned when he found the kitchen empty and nothing started for dinner.

Where on earth was she?

He vaguely recalled her saying something at breakfast about doing some Christmas shopping, but she should have been home by now. Normally, dinner would almost be ready to go on the table when he arrived from work. But nothing was cooking in the oven or the crockpot. He glanced around the kitchen. She hadn't left a note for him either. He couldn't remember the last time she'd gone somewhere without leaving a message for him. True, he'd gotten home a little earlier than usual but not that much earlier.

Where could she be?

As he studied the tidy room, he noticed the light flashing on the answering machine. Snow had fallen all afternoon, and the roads were starting to get sloppy. Syl had probably gotten stuck in traffic and had called the house to leave him a message. He rubbed his hands together—he really needed to get out his winter gloves—then measured grounds into the coffee brewer to make a warm drink. When the drink was ready, he cupped it in one hand and jabbed the playback bar on the answering machine with the other.

The voice that filled the kitchen definitely was not Sylvia's.

"Ah, Sylvia. It is Etienne," the smooth baritone proclaimed. "I am so disappointed you are not there. These carols playing on the radio have made me so lonely, and I knew talking to you would cheer me. But, *alors* that is not to be."

A deep sigh issued from the machine.

Dave shook his head in disgust. "Drama Queen!" he muttered.

"Have you thought more about our next trip, *cherie?*" the voice continued. "Eet would be wonderful to see you again. I have missed you. Eet has been too long. Call me, *s'il vous plait*, and let me know what you have decided. You have my number. I will be waiting."

Dave pressed the replay button and listened to the message again and then another time. With each playing, his anger deepened.

So this was why Sylvia wanted to go on all those trips. Was this phony Frenchman the reason she'd taken on so many students to tutor? So she could afford to go on trips with him? And where did this character get off anyway, calling another man's wife and leaving messages in that smarmy French accent?

Does the guy plan to replace me? Dave wondered.

When he'd picked Sylvia up from her bus trip, Dave had only gotten a brief glimpse of the man. This Etienne character had looked like he was barely half his wife's age. Well, maybe not *that* young, but definitely younger than Sylvia.

Dave carried his coffee into the den, swirling the dark brew thoughtfully as he walked. Was that why Syl suddenly decided to start walking at the Y and had her hair and nails done every week? He turned off the lamp then plopped down in his favorite chair to think.

What on earth had happened to his marriage? Sylvia hadn't been the same since she'd retired and suddenly gotten this bug to travel. Dave remembered the early days of their marriage when they'd been so in love. When Syl had told him she wanted to travel one day, Dave had promised to whisk her away for a long vacation once their kids were grown and they had money in the bank. He would have promised her the moon if it would make her smile.

Syl seemed to understand and never minded that they were poor. She believed him when he vowed to make a good life for them. And he had made good on that promise. He'd built a stable life for them, balanced on the twin pillars of Financial Security and Dependability. It was what Grandfather Beaumont had drilled into Dave's head all his life. Dave would have been more comfortable staying in a low-level job with his spreadsheets and actuary tables, but he'd advanced through the ranks at Davis Andrews to provide for his wife and children. Dave made a good salary but never spent a cent without first analyzing if the purchase was necessary. Their personal funds were invested even more carefully than those of his business clients. When the boys were born, he'd set aside money for their educations. He'd done the same for Lynne but had also started a wedding account for her. He and Sylvia owned a lovely home, drove nice cars, and were largely debt-free, thanks to his sensible money management. If his parents had been half as sensible, they would never have left their children penniless when they'd died.

Sensible.

Why did the word suddenly echo in his head like an accusation?

****

"Dave? Where are you?"

The sound of his wife's voice startled Dave awake. Before he could answer, the light flipped on in the den, half-blinding him.

"Why are you sitting here in the dark?"

Dave shrugged. "I dozed off."

He rubbed his eyes and stretched then glanced back over at his wife.

"Your boyfriend called," he said, watching her face for her reaction.

"My *what*?"

"Your travel friend. Englebert."

"Etienne?"

"Whatever." Dave brushed aside the correction. "He had some questions for you about your next trip. I didn't know you were planning to go away again."

"I told you about it, Dave. There's a concert of 60s and 70s music in January near the casino in Traverse City. I wanted more information before I signed up. I wasn't sure if you'd be able to come with me."

"It didn't sound like he was planning on me joining you, *cherie*. Anyway, the message is still on the machine. He said you have his number—or else it's probably on the caller ID." He felt the anger rising again and took a deep breath to try to calm down. He didn't want to argue with Sylvia, but knew he would if he stayed there. Dave rose from his chair and picked up his empty coffee cup. "I'll give you some privacy so you can call Eduardo back."

"Etienne," Sylvia corrected then puffed out a breath. "Anyway, there's no need for you to leave. I can call him later. I brought home pizza since I was so late. It'll take just a minute to set the table."

"I'm not hungry."

"But it's your favorite: pepperoni and portabellas on a thin crust."

"Doesn't matter," he said. "I'm going to bed."

Chapter Twenty

"No."

"No? But you've always liked the Londoners and—"

"It's too expensive and too soon after the holidays."

"It's not nearly as expensive as the historical tour I told you about. Nor as long as the one I told you I'd like to make to the Texas Quilt Museum someday. Besides, I'm making good money with my tutoring, honey. I have more than enough to pay for our tickets, the bus fares, and—"

"No. N. O. No!" he declared. The silverware rattled as he slammed his coffee mug on the breakfast table. "Or maybe I need to say *non* in some sissified French accent in order for you to listen to me."

Sylvia stared with shock at the man sitting across from her. She knew Dave had been upset over Etienne's message the night before. She'd been upset about it, too. The Londoners were Dave's favorites, so Sylvia had hoped the concert would entice him to make the trip with her. Etienne's call had pretty much shot that possibility. So she was angry, too. However, Dave's mood went way beyond angry. In all their years together, she'd never seen him quite like this. She sipped her coffee, took a deep breath, then tried to reason with him again.

"What about a different trip after the holidays, honey? Just you and me. We can go by car if you don't want to take a bus. It might be a lot of fun. We can pick some spot on the map and just take off."

"Doesn't interest me."

"Blast it, Dave!" she exclaimed, losing her patience. "What *does* interest you these days?"

"Getting this house fixed up so we can sell it."

"Sell the house?" She carefully set her mug down so he wouldn't notice her trembling hands then stared at him across the table. "Why would we want to sell our home?"

Dave shrugged. "It's too big. We don't need a four-bedroom house anymore. We need to downsize."

"I see." Her eyes narrowed, but she forced herself to keep an even voice. Screaming wouldn't help this situation. "And when did you plan to let me in on this decision, David? Before or after you started packing?"

He fidgeted in his chair, refusing to meet her eyes. "If you're going to be traipsing around the world, it won't really matter what kind of place you come home to. Besides, I figured you'll need more money for all your travels."

"*You* figured this? Based on the *one* trip I've made since retiring? Get real! I earned enough money for that trip as well as the next ones I wanted *us* to take *together*. I haven't taken one single, solitary cent from you—or from *my* retirement checks. Did you forget that little fact?"

He sighed. "I know. But—"

She continued as if he hadn't spoken, forcing herself to maintain a calm tone. "Dave, this is what we've talked about for years. Why we've always wanted to retire early."

"I don't."

"Don't what?"

"I don't want to retire, Sylvia. I have other plans."

Sylvia was glad she was sitting or her knees might have

given out. She knew things had been strained between them lately, but surely Dave wasn't talking about divorce. She wet her lips. "What do you mean by 'other plans'? What are you saying?"

"I've worked hard at Davis Andrews, Syl. I'm good at what I do, and our clients like me. But I've never risen higher than division manager."

"Honey, that's no reflection on you. Davis has always brought their vice-presidents in from the corporate headquarters in Atlanta."

"True. But that thinking has changed. Do you remember Roger Bentley?"

"The Grand Rapids VP? Of course. We went to the big welcome bash they threw for his family. It was just before Thanksgiving last year, and we had an early snowstorm. Remember how his wife kept looking out the window and saying it was like being inside a big snow globe? She couldn't wait to take their kids sledding."

"Well, apparently she changed her mind after a few months of the stuff. She told Roger she wasn't going through another winter like that. She took the kids and moved back to Atlanta before the school year started."

"Oh no. I'm so sorry to hear that. Are they divorcing...over a job?"

"When she left, Roger didn't know what would happen between them. I had drinks with him a few times after work—some of the nights when I got home late—he thought Joyce might file. But Joyce is the daughter of Michael Davis—"

"The CEO of your company?"

Dave nodded. "Apparently, Joyce blamed her father for the split. Said it was unforgivable of him to uproot families and move them to strange towns just to run a regional office. She said the branches already had plenty of qualified people who could run them. She must have made a pretty strong case, because Roger's been transferred back to Atlanta. I hear HR has contacted the vice-presidents at our other branches to see who else might want to move back to corporate."

"So who will run your branch now?"

"I'm not sure..." he hedged, looking everywhere except at her.

"Wait a minute. Did they offer you the job?"

"Not yet," he said. He took a sip of coffee then continued. "But Davis's assistant called yesterday. He wants to do a phone interview with me next week."

The more Dave talked, the more enthusiastic he became about the possibility. Sylvia listened and tried to make supportive comments, but she couldn't stop wondering how long this had been in the works and why she was only just now hearing about it. Of course, they really hadn't been talking too much about anything lately.

"So, that's all I know," Dave finished, holding his hands out, palms up. "Now, do you understand why I don't want to retire?"

"I do and I don't," Sylvia replied. "I understand you're excited about this opportunity—and you deserve the promotion. I'm happy for you. I really am..."

"But?" Dave asked and Sylvia could see his jaw tighten.

She clenched her hands in her lap and took a deep breath before answering. "But what about us?" she finally asked. "What about our plans? I told you how much I wanted to travel. For goodness sake, I've never been anywhere further than Grand Haven. I told you I couldn't even go on my senior trip because I had to take care of my mother..."

"Sylvia, you want to travel, I don't."

"You talked about it, too, Dave. You even analyzed how early we could retire without hurting our pensions..."

"Well, things have changed. I've changed. This is a chance of a lifetime for me. You don't seem to understand that."

"Oh, I understand it just fine!" Sylvia rose from her chair

and glared at her husband. "You've already made up your mind. You plan to accept the promotion when it's offered, scrap our retirement plans, and continue to invest for a someday that's so far in the future you'll probably never live to see it.

"What I do not see, David Miller, is any place for *me* in your high and mighty plans."

Chapter Twenty-One

He didn't want to be there.

Dave nursed his drink, listening with half an ear to the conversations buzzing around him, and wished he could be somewhere else. He hated these company parties where all the employees sucked up to the brass, and all the brass tried to act like they were just regular guys. He'd much rather be home in the den, watching this favorite Friday night line-up on their big screen TV.

Not Sylvia. She stood near the condo's fireplace, chatting easily with one of the company execs. Firelight shimmered on her deep blue silky dress, a dress that hugged every one of her shapely curves. Syl always looked forward to the Christmas party. When the invitation arrived in the mail, she'd immediately put it on their calendar and began planning what to wear.

Sylvia loved parties of every sort. He wouldn't call her a social butterfly; she just enjoyed people and was comfortable in these situations. He'd never met anyone like her. She could make polite conversation with anyone, from the new kid in the mailroom to the president of the company. Wherever she went in the room, people welcomed her with warm hugs and genuine smiles. DA's management should take lessons from her.

Maybe she could add lessons in social chitchat to her tutoring resume. She'd make a fortune. I could be her first student.

Dave had never learned the art of polite art of social conversation. His grandfather had considered parties a waste of money and energy. He'd raised Dave to speak only when he had something of value to say. Over the years, Sylvia had tried to assure him he had lots of important ideas to contribute to conversations. With her at his side, he'd slowly become a bit more self-assured both socially and in the accounting offices of Davis Andrews. Once he began to speak up at client meetings, people took notice, and he'd soon been given some big accounts to manage. However, he was always glad to have Sylvia by his side at important dinners and social events.

Tonight, it was more important than ever to mingle and pretend he was having a great time. Since Roger had returned to Atlanta, management had a VP position to fill, and Dave wanted his chance to reach for the brass ring. Vice-president. Head of the entire Midwest operation. His grandfather would have been pleased with that. Dave frowned and took another sip of his drink. *Actually, Grandfather would probably have found something wrong with it. Just as he did with everything else in my life.*

The thought shocked Dave. Did he really believe his grandfather had disapproved of him so deeply? A peal of familiar laughter floated across the room, disrupting Dave's introspection. He glanced around the room looking for its source, and spotted his wife with a group of DA's management, laughing at something Brian Dylan had said. Dave felt a twinge of jealousy as the company president put a hand on Sylvia's arm then leaned toward her to whisper something in her ear. She gave him one of her incandescent smiles but shook her head and turned to one of the other execs. Was the company president flirting with his wife?

Dave could hardly fault the man if he was. His petite wife looked gorgeous this evening. Her eyes sparkled and the champagne she'd been sipping brought a delightful glow to her cheeks. She was beautiful—as breathtaking as the day he'd married her—maybe more so. She'd swept back her dark hair in a twisty arrangement at the back of her head that showed off her long, graceful neck. All night long, he'd wanted to lean down and kiss that creamy skin and whisper, "I can't wait to get you home."

But he couldn't...she was leaving him.

His morose thoughts were interrupted by a delicate hand, stroking his arm. "So, how is our future vice-president doing this lovely evening?"

****

All evening, Sylvia had been circulating, trying to be the perfect corporate wife, but she was ready to go home. Dave hadn't mentioned the D word yet or made any further comments about selling the house since his outburst earlier in the week. Was stress over the job the reason behind his recent bouts of temper? If this promotion meant that much to him, she planned to do everything she could to help further his cause.

Determined to show Dave her support, she'd spent the morning at the beauty shop—the day spa they called it now—having her hair tinted then arranged in an elegant braided updo. She'd even splurged on a facial. Weeks before, she'd spotted the perfect cocktail dress in a small shop near The Stitching Post. Dave loved sapphire blue, so she'd bought the beautiful column dress even though it had been a bit snug around her hips. However, last night, she'd tried it on, and the dress had skimmed her figure beautifully. All that walking had really paid off. Or maybe it had been her loss of appetite from worrying about her marriage. Whatever the cause, she knew she looked her best. In fact, Lynne had stopped by the house and had raved about her sexy new look.

But Dave hadn't noticed. Before they'd left the house, he had barely glanced at her outfit even though she was wearing the strappy stiletto heels he always found so sexy.

Since arriving at the party, he'd left her to fend for herself while he chatted with the group of execs standing near the bar. In her head, Sylvia knew he had to mix and mingle with the people who could influence his promotion. But couldn't he have taken a few seconds to comment on her appearance? Other men certainly had. One of Dave's half-inebriated coworkers kept making embarrassing passes, and Brian Dylan, DA's president, flirted outrageously every time he came near her. In the past, Dave would have noticed when men hit on her, and he would have come to stand protectively beside her.

Tonight, he didn't seem to care. He hadn't commented on her appearance or the fact that she wore his favorite color. Etienne certainly would have noticed. Her gallant Canadian friend would have lavished compliments on her elegant hairdo, and he definitely would have had something to say about her sexy shoes.

Didn't Dave care about her anymore? They had always had such an intense, physical intimacy. Nowadays, he forgot to kiss her goodnight half the time. When he did remember, the kiss was barely a peck on the cheek.

She closed her eyes for a moment, thinking about the upcoming holidays. What if Dave was merely waiting for them to pass before he served her with divorce papers? Her stomach suddenly lurched. How on earth could she get through their family gatherings without letting the kids see her worry? She needed to get away, needed time to think. Maybe she should go to the concert after all. It might be hard listening to the Londoners perform the songs she and Dave had loved, but the time away would give her time to think, to decide what to do about her marriage.

"Do you want something more?"

The question jerked Sylvia back to her festive surroundings. She opened her eyes in time to see a slender redhead in a low cut, too-tight, mini dress lean against Dave as she laughingly retrieved her drink from the bar behind him.

Sylvia turned toward the young waiter, who'd asked the question. He extended a tray filled with champagne flutes toward her.

"Do you want something more?" he repeated.

"Oh, I do indeed. But nothing you have on your tray."

Chapter Twenty-Two

"Honey, did you get the extra batteries for the camera?"

Sylvia didn't wait for an answer. In the mood he was in, Dave would answer when he got around it, but she didn't have time that morning to try to jolly him into a better mood. The kids were coming for brunch, and she wanted everything to be perfect. The baked omelet was warming in the oven, the coffee pot was filled and ready to brew, and all the juices were chilled. Croissants and Danishes rested in separate, napkin-lined baskets. Now it was time to set the table. At the last moment, Sylvia decided to splurge and use her good china.

Dave shuffled into the kitchen, holding a new package of batteries. "Got the batteries right here. I don't know why you need to take pictures every single year. It's the same bunch of people in the same place, doing the same things each time. We just get older in each set of pictures. Besides, if the batteries run out, the kids all have cameras on their phones."

Sylvia suppressed a sigh. A few months ago, she might have laughed at her endearing curmudgeon, now the tension between them made it an effort not to criticize him for being Scrooge. But this was Christmas Day. The children would arrive soon, and she was going to try her hardest to put on a cheerful face for them.

She pushed back a lock of hair that had fallen over her eyes. Her new haircut was going to take some getting used to. So was the color. It was a subtle change, but with the gray covered, she felt younger, more energetic. The salon had been running a special on manicures, and she'd splurged on that, too. She could count on one hand the number of professional manicures she'd had in her lifetime. It had been an expense she just couldn't justify when they were raising their kids and getting financially stable. But now, the kids were out of the house and she didn't need to be so frugal. Besides, she'd picked up some additional tutoring, too. A few university students had needed coaching, and she'd made some extra money that way. So she deserved a day of pampering, and she felt soft and feminine from head to toe.

D2 arrived first. He came in through the garage door, set his boots on the mat in the mudroom, and hung his coat up. So meticulous, just like his father. He made sure everything was hung neatly before coming into the kitchen to give his mother a warm hug. "Merry Christmas, Mom."

"Merry Christmas, Davey," she replied, reverting to his childhood name as she hugged him back. "How were the roads from Chicago?"

"Not bad at all. We got an early start in order to avoid the traffic, but the plows had already been out, and the roads were clear."

"That's great. But where's your brother? Didn't he come with you?"

"Oh, you know John. As soon as he got out of the car he spied Mrs. Carruthers getting her morning paper next door, and he had to rush over to talk to her."

Her younger son had always been the more social of the two boys. "I'm sure Leona enjoyed that. Meanwhile, could you help me finish setting the table?"

Lynne and Ron arrived with a large tray of fruit just as the last place was set. Dave took their coats, Ron put their gifts under the tree, and the family sat down to eat.

"Mom, you look so different. I love what they did to your hair," Lynne remarked.

D2 peered at her. "I thought something was different about you. It's darker, isn't it? Or maybe it just looks that way with all the gray gone. It's a lot nicer this way."

Lynne swatted her brother. "You oaf. No wonder you're still single. Don't you know you should never tell a woman how gray she used to be? Just tell her how young she looks now."

The children laughed, but Sylvia noticed Dave hadn't said a word. With his head down, he concentrated on cutting his food into uniformly sized morsels.

Doesn't he like my new look?

Well, too bad. She wasn't going to dwell on him and his odd moods. The kids were not going to see her worrying about her marriage on Christmas. She would be the happy mom and loving wife they were used to seeing. And hopefully, as soon as Dave opened his gift from her, she hoped he'd realize how supportive she now was of his plan to keep working. It had taken her a long time to find a special gift that would tell him, but she'd finally found a beautiful monogrammed desk set for him. She remembered seeing a similar set once on his grandfather's desk, and since he revered his Grandpa Beaumont, she decided to outfit him with a similar set. It had cost more than they usually spent on gifts for each other, but she'd had her extra tutoring money, so she could easily afford the luxury.

****

Dave tried to keep his expression pleasant, but he could feel the heat rising in his ears. He knew if his kids took a close look at him, they'd notice his red neck and cheeks. Blast it, he'd wanted to compliment Sylvia on her appearance, but the kids had beaten him to it.

Now, hearing her thank them and say how much younger it made her feel, he regretted not speaking up. In his opinion, Syl hadn't needed to dye her hair or get a new haircut. She was already the most attractive woman of her age he knew. Shoot, she was the most attractive woman he knew, period. Those yahoos at the company party sure hadn't been able to keep their eyes off her. Why didn't she realize how beautiful she was?

He sighed. Maybe he hadn't told her enough recently. *Have I told her at all lately?* He wanted to kick himself for not telling her how nice she'd looked that morning. Now, if he said anything, it would look like he was doing it only because the kids had said something. If he was in the doghouse, he deserved to be. He used to tell her all the time, but recently, he'd been afraid to do so since he wasn't sure if she was doing it because of the Frenchman.

Besides, it seemed that lately anything he said came out wrong.

Well, hopefully she'd like his gift. It was something he'd seen her pick up in the store the last time they'd gone to the mall together. She'd put it back down, but he'd remembered it and gone back later to get it. He could hardly wait to see her face.

As was the custom on holidays in the Miller home, the men cleaned up after the meal since the women had prepared the food. While the boys rinsed off the dishes and put them in the dishwasher, Dave cleaned off the table and wiped it down then replaced the table runner and centerpiece. Finally they all migrated to the living room where the seven-foot tall Douglas fir presided. Since the kids no longer took part in decorating the tree, Sylvia had done it all herself this year. He wondered if she resented him for not helping her with the job this year.

They used to have such a great time decorating the tree together.

He settled in his chair, and waited as the others took their favorite seats on either the couch or floor. John volunteered to play Santa. As always, he clowned it up and presented every gift with a joke or a flourish. Sylvia, as always, had found perfect gifts for each of the kids. All of them, including his new son-in-law, were thrilled with what they'd received. A soft wool sweater and gloves for Lynne, NFL sweatshirts and warm gloves for the boys. And of course, each of the kids had received a stocking filled with candy, fruit, and silly gag gifts.

Sylvia always seemed to know just what to get, but getting a gift for her was tougher. Long ago, he'd learned he had to do it himself. Over the years, he'd tried to enlist the kids' help, but that hadn't worked too well. They'd always suggest things they liked for themselves. Asking her friends hadn't been a good idea, either. They couldn't keep secrets, and Sylvia had known what he'd gotten her long before she'd unwrapped the package. He had learned to watch her and get his clues from the way she acted. And he'd picked a winner this time. Now, if only everyone would dispense with all this chitchat. It wasn't like the kids had been gone for years. Dave's anxiety rose with each passing minute. When would they get to his gift?

"Dad?"

Dave blinked. John stood in front of him with a wide, flat box. He took it, noting the tag. It was from Syl.

"Come on, Dad, open it up," Lynne encouraged.

He slid the ribbon off and then picked off the tape, the way Grandpa Beaumont had taught him. If he was careful, the wrapping paper could be used again. The kids teased him about his frugality, but old habits were hard to break. Finally, he got to the gift itself. His eyes widened. It was a leather desk set, just like the one his grandfather had used. When Grandpa Beaumont had passed away Dave had inherited it and used it until it grew so worn he'd had to throw it out. He missed that set but had never bought a new one. How had she known?

"Merry Christmas, Mr. Vice-President," Syl said, giving him a big smile across the room.

"Thank you," he said, basking for a moment in the warmth of her smile.

Finally, John handed his mother a large shirt box. Dave grimaced at the store's fancy gift-wrappings. He'd hated to spend the extra money for the paper and bow, but he'd learned the hard way that the appearance of a gift was almost as important to Syl as what was inside. Since he couldn't decorate gifts nearly as well as his wife, he'd splurged. He held his breath as she pulled the ribbon off the package then carefully picked off the tape. He was glad to see she wanted to save the pretty paper, but a part of him wanted to tear off the paper himself so he could see her delighted reaction.

After what seemed ages, she opened the box and lifted out a high-necked, pink flannel nightgown and held it up.

Silence. No one said a word. The kids looked from their mother to him as if waiting for something to happen. What was wrong?

"Oh, how pretty," Sylvia finally said. She placed it carefully back in the box. "It's... a lovely color and will...definitely keep me warm this winter."

Dave felt his insides start to boil. What had gone wrong? She'd gushed over the gifts the kids brought her, and they were nothing but gift cards. Lynne had gotten her some little trinket to hang over the kitchen window—a colored glass sign that said something about *Home is Where the Heart is* or some nonsense like that. This nightgown had cost a lot more than that sign. And it was functional, too. Why couldn't Syl appreciate that? Besides, she'd wanted it. That's what she was trying to tell him when she didn't buy it, right?

"That's the one you picked up when we were at the mall a few weeks ago. I thought you liked it."

Her mouth curved upward, though Dave noted her eyes lacked the sparkle they always got when she was truly happy about something. "I do like it, Dave. Thank you for noticing that I'd admired it at the mall." She turned back to the kids.

"So, what else did Santa get you?" The perkiness in her voice seemed a little forced, but the kids filled in the gap with their answers.

Dave tuned out the conversation. Heavy hearted, he realized he'd somehow messed up again.

The long day loomed before him.

Chapter Twenty-Three

Another year. How many New Year's Eve shows had she watched over the years? Sylvia wondered. Dick Clark had been in his prime when she and Dave had cuddled on their second-hand couch for their first New Year's together. They'd gotten so wrapped up in each other that they had almost missed seeing the ball drop. Now, the passion in their marriage had departed as finally as Dick Clark had, leaving nothing behind but memories.

Another unfamiliar music group took to the stage to perform. Since she didn't particularly like their music, she got up to refill her glass with champagne. Raising the glass toward the television, she gave a mock toast: "To another year of hopes and dreams being dashed against the rocks."

Why on earth was she being so melodramatic tonight? she thought as she made her way back to the couch. *Just because Dave decided to go to bed early doesn't mean I have to let it ruin my evening.*

Before she sat down, her cell phone gave a muted ring. Thinking it might be one of the kids, she raced to find it. The thing was buried somewhere in her purse. Where had it gone?

Ah, there it was, under the stack of Christmas receipts.

She connected with a breathy "Hello?"

"*Bonsoir*, Sylvia."

"Etienne?"

"*Mais oui, cherie. Bonne année et bonne santé.* Good year and good health."

"Thank you, Etienne. Happy New Year to you, also."

"*Merci.* I wanted to call to find out if you had decided to go on the concert bus trip. I need a seatmate, *cherie*. Please say you will come and keep me company, *non*?"

Sylvia chuckled. "Good grief, Etienne, I'm sure there will be no shortage of women who will be more than happy to keep you company."

"Ah, but none are as lovely and charming as you."

"You flatter me," she protested but wondered if he could hear the smile in her voice. "But, I'm still not sure, Etienne. The weather can be vicious up north in January, especially along Lake Michigan. The roads get quite treacherous. I don't want to be on a bus when it's icy."

"If the weather is bad, I am certain Traveling Solo will cancel or reschedule the trip. But if the roads are clear, we could have a marvelous trip, *non*? The concert has been getting wonderful reviews, and you said you wanted to see The Londoners. So, please, call Deanna and sign up."

"Well…The Londoners *are* one of my favorite groups, and I really wanted to see them in concert, but Dave still doesn't want to go…"

She paused and looked at the TV where happy partygoers huddled in Times Square and watched the New Year ball slowly descend. They looked as cold as she felt inside.

"Okay, Etienne," she said. "I'll think about it."

"Please do not just think about eet, *cherie*. Say yes. The trip will not be the same without your lovely presence."

"That is very charming, Etienne." She chuckled. Surely,

he didn't think she'd be taken in by his outrageous flattery. However, she had to admit, it felt nice to have someone make the effort.

"So you will make the trip with me?"

"I will *consider* it," she clarified. "Happy New Year, Etienne."

****

Dave stood in the hallway, unable to believe what he'd just heard. He'd been unable to sleep and had noticed the time on the bedside clock. He knew Sylvia had been disappointed that he hadn't stayed up to watch the annual broadcast from Times Square, so he'd gotten up to wish her Happy New Year. But his wife didn't seem to be all that unhappy now. Had he just heard her actually making a date with the smarmy Frenchman?

He watched her as she disconnected and put her phone back in her purse. She did a little pirouette, like their daughter used to do when she'd gotten off the phone with whatever boy she was dating at the time. His wife's step seemed a little wobbly to Dave. Did the man affect her that way, putting her off balance? The real test was her expression. She'd always had such an expressive face he could tell what she was thinking just by looking at her eyes.

He stepped into the family room to get a better look.

"Oh, Dave! You startled me. I thought you'd gone to bed for the night." Sylvia's flushed face and gleaming eyes told him a story he'd hoped he wouldn't read.

"I did go to bed, but I noticed it was midnight. I got up to wish you Happy New Year, but I see your Frenchman beat me to it. Are you planning to see him soon?"

He was surprised when Sylvia didn't bother correcting him again about the man's nationality. "I might. I told you about the trip to the concert."

"And you also told me you probably wouldn't go because of the unpredictable weather. I take it Etienne changed your mind?"

"I don't see what difference that makes to you. You weren't going to go with me anyway."

"Maybe not, but I didn't expect my wife to go with another man!"

"Oh stop it. You know it's not like that! Etienne has always been a perfect gentleman."

"For now. The man is merely biding his time before he makes his move."

"You're being very unfair. You don't even know Etienne. Besides, you have female friends at work. You even have lunch with other women."

"That's completely different. We're working, not sightseeing and going to concerts together."

"But people seeing you eating together might get a different impression."

"I have never done anything inappropriate."

"Are you saying I have?" Her blue eyes flashed daggers at him.

"I'm saying—I don't know what to think." He stormed over to the closet and pulled out his winter coat and boots, putting them on over his pajamas. "I need to go out and walk."

"At midnight on New Year's?"

"What difference does it make to you? You've got travel plans to make."

He zipped up his coat, jammed his hat on his head, and opened the door. A blast of cold air almost made him reconsider, but he was too angry to face Sylvia again without saying something he'd regret later.

****

A heavy, wet snow had been falling since mid-afternoon, and the front walk was slippery, but Dave kept going until he got to the driveway then followed it to the sidewalk. He paused momentarily, unsure which way to head. Whenever he walked for exercise, he usually went to the park and followed the foot trails. The same trails Sylvia had visited so often before the cold weather had prevented it. She'd claimed walking helped her get more toned and increased her energy level. But now, he wondered if she'd had an ulterior motive. Had she really wanted to get healthier, or had she wanted to look better for the Frenchman?

He crossed the road then stopped. Going to the park at this hour probably wouldn't be a smart thing to do. Grandville was a nice enough suburb, but it would be foolish to take a chance. Instead, he headed downtown, where a couple of all night businesses would still be open. Maybe, he could waste a little time in the convenience store and buy a cup of coffee to warm up.

Rats! Dave patted his pants and realized he didn't have his wallet with him. Worse yet, he wasn't even dressed. If he'd walked into the store dressed in pajamas and a winter jacket, he'd cause quite the commotion. Dave detested being the center of attention. Especially when he was the butt of a joke.

The damp snow soaked the hem of his cotton pajama bottoms, and his legs were getting cold. Sadly, he turned around and headed back home. If he was lucky, maybe Sylvia had gone to bed, and he could spend the rest of the night in front of the television. He'd certainly done that enough the last few months, but it was a miserable way to start the New Year. Suddenly, he recalled the festive midnight meals his parents had always served in front of the TV on New Year's Eve. Sparkling punch, cookies, and platters of delicious meats and cheeses. They'd laugh and feast, and his mother would remind them "How you begin the New Year is also how you will end it."

A shuddering chill suddenly ran through him, clutching at his heart. The chill had nothing to do with the weather and everything to do with his wife.

Is more fighting and anger the best we can expect his year? Instead of a bright New Year, is this the end for us?

Chapter Twenty-Four

On the morning of the concert, Sylvia awoke a few minutes before her alarm went off. She quickly reached over and turned off the buzzer so it wouldn't disturb Dave's sleep. Since his promotion, he'd worked late most nights and would spend a couple more hours in his home office after a hurried and mostly silent dinner. That had become the norm for them since their argument on New Year's Eve, but last night, he'd come to bed long after she'd settled in for the night. Since Saturday was the one day a week when he could actually sleep in, she carefully slid out from beneath the covers.

It was dark in the bedroom, but after so many years in this house, she didn't need a light to navigate through any of the rooms. She tiptoed to the chair where she'd laid out her clothes the previous night, gathered up everything she needed, and slipped out the bedroom door. After carefully closing the door, she set her things on the vanity in the second bathroom then headed to the kitchen for a much-needed cup of coffee.

Before starting the brewer, Sylvia walked over to the sliding door and peered through the glass. The TV8 weatherman had predicted snow during the night, but she was relieved to see only a dusting on the lawn and trees. As she'd told Etienne, Michigan's winters were unpredictable, and she worried about taking a trip to the northern part of the state in January. Despite his coaxing, she'd refused to commit to go. However, the chance to see the Londoners live had been too tempting to miss, so she'd finally called Deanna and made the arrangements just a few days ago. Luckily, Traveling Solo had still had a ticket available.

The heavenly smell of coffee drew her away from the slider. Grateful the snow wasn't as bad as had been predicted, she picked up her mug and blew on the hot beverage. *Mmm,* she thought as she savored the first sip. *Forget about wine, coffee is the true nectar of the gods.* She took a couple more swallows then reluctantly put down the mug to go and get ready.

A hot shower chased away the last remnants of sleepiness. Sylvia lingered under the spray for a few extra minutes, grateful her low-maintenance, chin-length hair wouldn't need more than a couple shots of the blow dryer to be ready. After drying off, she dressed in a simple ivory sweater and her favorite pair of jeans. She'd chosen the outfit in order to be comfortable on the long bus trip but had to admit it looked pretty flattering, too. A touch of eye shadow and she was good to go. Lipstick could wait until after she had a second cup of coffee.

She was surprised to find Dave in the kitchen, fully dressed, when she returned there.

"I hope I didn't wake you," she apologized. "I tried to be quiet—"

"Why didn't you wake me?" he asked in an accusing tone.

"You were up late...I thought you'd want to sleep in."

"How were you going to get to the high school?"

Why did his words make her feel like she had to defend herself? She hadn't done anything wrong. "I planned to drive my car. That way you won't have to worry about picking me up tonight. We might—"

"Or maybe you just don't want me around. Were you in such a rush to see your boyfriend that you planned to leave without even telling me goodbye?

"What? Of course not. I'd never leave without saying—" She stopped, suddenly realizing what he'd implied.

"David, I keep telling you, Etienne is not my—"

"That's what you keep telling me," he interrupted in a weary voice, "but—"

"But what?" she asked, sensing he had more to say. Then she noticed how pale and tired he appeared. Had his new job already taken such a big toll of him?

He opened his mouth to answer then sighed and merely shook his head. "I'll get the car," he said then strode from the room.

What on earth is the matter with that man? Sylvia wondered as the outside door slammed behind him. A tightening across her temples announced the beginnings of a colossal headache. She reached into the cabinet for the bottle of aspirin she kept there.

If Dave keeps this up, she thought as she swallowed down a couple of tablets with the dregs of her coffee, *I'm going to need to buy an aspirin factory.*

Chapter Twenty-Five

She'd actually done it.

Dave stood in the school parking lot and watched as the Traveling Solo bus pulled out of the drive and turned toward the highway. He couldn't believe it. Sylvia had gone to the concert without him. After all these years, his wife preferred the company of a bunch of strangers to being with him. Or were they strangers? Dave saw the guy who'd quickly stood up when Sylvia got on the bus. Dark, wavy hair, lean build. He was sure it was the Frenchman. Emile or Eduard or whatever the Dickens his name was. The guy who'd been on the first trip with Sylvia and had given her the black eye. The same Lothario who had been calling her at least once a week since then. Sylvia said Etienne—that was his name—was just a friend. But was he?

Dave recalled the numerous messages the man had left on the answering machine as well as the phone calls—including the one on New Year's Eve—he had made to Sylvia. After that one, they hadn't really spoken much to each other. Dave had found countless excuses to stay late at the office, and on the nights he was home, he'd usually head to his office to do paperwork. He wanted to talk to her, wanted to put things back on track with her, but had no idea how to go about it. Everything he did or said seemed to only make things worse.

Frustrated, Dave kicked a clod of snow across the parking lot as he went back to his SUV. The weatherman had predicted snow that afternoon, and the dark clouds in the sky seemed to agree with the forecast. They looked as gloomy as he felt. He slipped into the driver's seat then sat for a moment with his hands resting on the steering. What was he supposed to do on a winter afternoon while his wife was off frittering away money on a concert and shopping? He hated to think how much Sylvia had spent for a few hours of pleasure.

Oh well. It was *her* money. She had earned it with her tutoring, so she could blow it however she wanted, but a prudent woman would have added it to her retirement fund. But maybe prudence wasn't what Sylvia needed at the moment. He recalled their conversation about her mother's illness and her father's denial of it. That had to have been hard on a kid barely in her teens. Their deaths so close together and the guilt she'd felt about them would have flattened most people, but Syl had not only survived, she'd succeeded. He wished she had told him long ago about the feelings she'd kept bottled up inside herself.

And what would you have done? his conscience asked. *Syl told you all she'd ever wanted was the chance to travel and see a bit of the state. And what did you do? You lectured her about squandering money foolishly. Even this morning, seeing her off, you were more worried about the money she was spending than the fact that another man had designs on her.*

Dave shook his head. Sylvia would never cheat on him. She had too much integrity to betray her marriage vows.

So what's to stop her from divorcing you?

Dave puffed out a breath. *How had it come to this?*

When they were newly married, they were so crazy in love. They hadn't needed money or possessions to be happy.

They did countless things together on weekends. Picnics in the park, arts and crafts shows, visits to the zoo. Sylvia discovered a love of quilting, and he found pleasure gardening.

They'd shared passion and intimacy, raised a family, planned a future. Together. But would Sylvia be around to share that future now or would she leave him like his parents had?

His parents? Where had that come from?

Irritated at himself for opening that particular door, he started the car to head for home. However, when he reached the exit of the school parking lot, he knew he couldn't face that big empty house right then. He checked the road for traffic then signaled a turn and headed in the opposite direction.

****

"She's leaving me."

Muriel's head popped up from beneath the counter where she'd been rummaging for a baking dish. She frowned at her youngest brother. "Good grief, David. You can't possibly be serious."

Dave pulled out the nearest chair and sank into it. His sister's antique kitchen set wasn't exactly made for comfort. You couldn't really sink into it as much as perch on it. But he didn't care; he slumped into the seat. "I wish I weren't serious, Mure. But I am."

She straightened up, leaned against the counter, then folded her arms across her slight chest. "Do you want to talk about it? Tell me what happened."

He shook his head sadly. "That's just it, I'm not sure if I can. I don't know what happened. It's like Sylvia is a different person. Ever since Lynne's wedding, all she talks about is going on trips. She wants to travel here, there, everywhere. She already went on one bus trip last fall, and she's on another today. She plans to go on more of them, too. She's meeting new people, and she wants to socialize with them between trips."

"And what's so wrong with that, David?"

"Money." He shrugged as if the one word explained everything.

"Oh dear, I'm so sorry. Is she spending money that's supposed to pay your bills? Do you need a loan?"

He frowned as if his sister was speaking a foreign language. "No, of course not."

"Then how *is* Sylvia paying for these trips?" She pinned him with a piercing look that tolerated no half-truths.

"Remember we told you she's been coaching kids after school? She uses the money she earns from her tutoring."

"Not her pension money or funds from your savings?"

Dave shook his head.

"So what exactly is the problem? Is Sylvia behaving inappropriately on the trips? Are the people she travels with disreputable?"

"No, there are a lot of retirees, and a few young people, but most are middle-aged and older. Some are widows or widowers or folks whose spouses can't get away to travel with them. They call their group Traveling Solo, which sounds like they're a bunch of swinging singles, but they aren't."

He frowned. "Well, except for some Romeo who keeps calling Syl all the time."

Muriel's spine stiffened. "Are you telling me that Sylvia is having an affair?"

"No!" He paused then scratched his head. "At least, I don't think so. Not yet."

"Yet?"

Muriel's stare made Dave squirm just as it always had. The former principal had spent her career dealing with moody teenagers. A single look could worm the truth out of even the most stubborn of them. Her glare had the power to make men quake.

"I don't know." Dave got up and paced. Or tried to. He could cross Muriel's small kitchen in four-and-a-half steps.

"Has she been coming on to this man?" his sister continued the interrogation.

"No. At least not that I've seen. It's just that—" Dave paused and threw up his hands in exasperation. "He makes her all cheerful, opening doors for her, helping her with her bags, standing up when she gets on the bus."

"So he's a gentleman," Muriel clarified. "Those are things you were taught to do for women, too, aren't they?"

"I suppose," Dave muttered and slumped back down on the chair. "But he's—well—he's with her. He's making these trips with her and all."

"So, why don't you go, too?"

"I already told you, Mure. They cost money. M-O-N-E-Y."

"Exactly." His sister nodded as if he'd made her point. "Money that you have thanks to a good career. Two good careers, actually, since Sylvia has worked most of your marriage, too."

"Spending money on travel is frivolous. It's a flagrant waste!" he ranted. "What good is a trip going to be when we're old? Postcards and souvenirs won't buy us medicine or pay our doctor bills." He shook his head. "I refuse to end up like our mother and father."

"And *what* exactly was wrong with our parents?"

Dave didn't think he'd ever seen his sister look sterner or colder. He could almost see ice crystals forming in the air around her. "Um," he back peddled. "Well, nothing really, but—"

"But what?"

"Well, they left us paupers. Dependent on handouts from our relatives. I remember Grandpa complained when they died that there wouldn't even be enough money to bury them."

Muriel gave him a long, thoughtful look then shook her head, sadly. "Oh, Davey. I forgot how very young you were when Mom and Dad died. All those years you spent alone with Grandfather, he must have really warped your thinking."

"He took us in when no one else did," Dave insisted.

"Oh, honey, is that what you thought?" She sighed. "I knew Grandfather was a bitter and lonely old man, but I never realized how much nonsense he fed you. I'm sure Grandfather preached to you about hoarding every cent you earned. Did he also warn you that spending money for leisure activities was foolishness and would leave you destitute and dependent on others?

Dave nodded.

"I am so sorry," Muriel apologized. "Bill and I were stupid not to realize what he'd done to you."

"What do you mean?"

She leaned against the kitchen counter again, studying him for a moment. When she spoke, it was to ask a question of her own. "David, didn't you ever wonder how I was able to afford to finish college then go on to graduate school after our folks died? Or how Bill managed to do the same? And just where did you think the money for your own tuition came from?"

"Grandfather said—"

Muriel shook her head and held up a finger to silence him. "I need to show you something," she said. "Wait here."

She left the kitchen and went into the other room. He heard the sound of a drawer sliding open then closing again. A few moments later, his sister returned to the kitchen, carrying a large, lace-trimmed book. A faded, pink satin ribbon encircled it to hold it shut. Muriel stroked the padded fabric cover, and, for a moment, a soft smile transformed her stern features. Then she crossed the floor and stood in front of him, holding out the book to him with both hands.

"This is Mom's journal. She kept it from when she was a

young girl until she left with Dad on that last trip. I've treasured it all these years. It made me feel close to her, gave me insights into how she felt about life, the way she thought. I never realized you might need her words a lot more than I did.

"Take it home with you, Davey," she said in a gentle voice. "You need to read it, honey."

"I don't see what—"

"Take it." The brook-no-nonsense principal was back. She put the book in his hands and looked into his eyes. "Read it carefully. It will help you to know our parents. Maybe then you'll understand how things really were."

****

Dave came out of Muriel's house to see the snow had started in earnest. Fat flakes swirled and danced in the beams of his headlights, coming down harder as he neared home. The roads were going to be drifted over and icy if the snow kept coming down at the rate it now fell. He was glad to have good snow tires on his SUV as well as Sylvia's car. Dave hoped the Traveling Solo bus was equipped for the bad weather, too. Snowfall was always much worse along the shore of Lake Michigan, and northern towns like Traverse City often received more than twice the amount of inland towns downstate.

Their house was dark under the slate-covered sky, but the security lights turned on as soon as Dave pulled into the driveway. He briefly considered leaving the car in the driveway since he had to go out again in a few hours to pick up Sylvia when her bus returned. But putting the car in the garage would prevent him from having to brush it off—or maybe even scrape it off—later on, so he hit the remote for the garage and parked next to Sylvia's little compact.

As he unlocked the door between the garage and the kitchen, he remembered he'd left his mother's journal on the back seat. He sighed. He had absolutely no interest in reading it, didn't want to dredge up all those old emotions. But Mure would have his head if she found out he'd tossed it in the backseat and just left it there. With a sigh, he returned to the car and retrieved the frilly thing. He'd just put it in his office for a few days then return it to her. His sister didn't need to know he hadn't read it.

The kitchen felt cold and empty to Dave without Sylvia bustling around in it. He hung his keys on the rack by the door then went through to his office, flipping on lamps as he went. The light didn't make much improvement. The house still felt empty. *Funny how the absence of one person can make all the difference in the world.*

He missed her. He wondered what she was doing at that moment. *Was Sylvia having fun?* Part of him hoped his wife was having a wonderful time. She'd always loved The Londoners. In fact, when they were first married, Dave used to tease her about secretly being in love with the British group's lead singer, Bobby. Sylvia would just grin, hum the refrain from their hit song, *Can't Get Enough,* and snuggle against him. Last summer, she'd been so excited when he'd given her one of their CDs so she could listen to their music when she drove her car. Dave smiled, remembering how she'd laughed and hummed the familiar song then led him down the hall to their bedroom.

Confound it! What had gone wrong between the two of them?

Chapter Twenty-Six

"You've been a great crowd!" Bobby Marlette exclaimed at the conclusion of the band's show. "I'm not sure I'd have come out on such a beastly night just to see these blokes." He gestured at his band members. "But we're all mighty glad you did. Now, bundle up and be safe on the drive home."

Thundering applause filled the auditorium of the Traverse Bay Arena as the group took their final bow. Sylvia clapped as loudly as the rest of the audience as The Londoners exited from the stage. The British singers might be getting up in years, but they could still put on a dynamite show. Dave would have loved it. The group had performed all his favorite songs—*their* favorite songs: cheeky *Tattoo Rosie*, sultry *City Heat*, the driving bass of *Can't Get Enough*. The music had run like the soundtrack of her marriage, accompanying mental images of her and Dave as they'd talked, laughed, shared their dreams and disappointments, and made sweet passionate love.

Oh, Dave. I wish you had come with me, she thought as she stood up and prepared to leave.

"What was that, *cherie?*"

Etienne's question made her realize she'd spoken her thought out loud. Embarrassed, she shook her head and fumbled for her jacket. He reached over and took it from her, holding it gallantly so she could slip her arms into it.

"Eet was a good show, was eet not, *cherie*? You are not regretting your decision to come, are you?"

"Oh no, Etienne, The Londoners were wonderful, and this auditorium is absolutely beautiful."

"Very good." He nodded at her reply then tucked her arm through his and guided her toward the center aisle.

The rest of the group had made good progress toward the door; however, Etienne seemed in no hurry to join them. Every few feet, he stopped to let other audience members go ahead of them. Soon, he and Sylvia had fallen far behind their group. She fretted at the thought of keeping everyone waiting, but when she mentioned it to Etienne, he merely patted her arm.

"Do not worry. The bus, eet cannot leave without us. They will wait," he said as they traversed the long, carpeted hallway to the main lobby.

If his comment was meant to soothe her mind, it fell flat. Sylvia hated to keep people waiting. *Dave would have known that*, she thought and tried to hurry their pace. When they finally reached the rendezvous spot where most of their group waited, she saw Deanna and their bus driver, Carl, standing to one side of the lobby with their heads together.

"They don't look very happy," Sylvia remarked. "I wonder what's up." Tugging Etienne along, she hurried across the lobby to find out why everyone looked so grim.

"What is it? What's happened?"

Deanna motioned for everyone to gather around her then delivered the bad news. "I'm sorry, people, but the snow really dumped on us while we were in the concert." She pointed toward the windows where the falling snow made it impossible to see more than a few feet away.

"Carl's been listening to updates on the radio," she continued. "A big accident on US-31 south of here has the road blocked. The state police are warning everyone to stay off the roads except for emergencies."

"What does that mean?" one of the group, a man named Joe, voiced what the rest of them were thinking.

Deanna puffed out a breath. "It means we can't head back home tonight. It just wouldn't be safe."

"What will we do?"

"We can't spend the night on the bus."

"Where will we stay?"

As questions bombarded her, Deanna held up her hand for silence. "We have things covered. Carl's checked with the hotel desk here at the resort. They don't have enough vacant rooms to accommodate us individually, but can if we double up. It will be cheaper that way, too. Okay?"

When that seemed agreeable, she continued. "Good. I'll use our trip roster to pair you up. Listen for your names then go sign in at the desk. Sylvia, you'll be with me."

Sylvia nodded. "Okay, I'll get us registered while you assign the rest of the pairs."

****

"So we won't be able to get home until sometime tomorrow," Sylvia apologized on the phone. In the mood her husband had been in lately, she'd dreaded Dave's reaction to the news. He didn't disappoint her.

"I told you it was positively crazy to travel up north in January."

"And you were right," she admitted in a soothing voice. Leaning against the headboard of the bed, she settled in to tell him about the show. "But, honey, the concert was—"

"Call me when you get in so I'll know to pick you up," he interrupted then hung up before she could reply.

Sylvia sighed and pressed the end button on her cell phone. She set it down on the nightstand between the room's two double beds.

"Trouble in paradise?" Deanna asked. She stood in the bathroom door, brushing her long auburn hair.

"He's not too happy about the weather."

"None of us are. But I figure we need to just 'go with the flow.'" She winked and made air quotes with her fingers. "You going to 'flow on' down to the bar and meet your Frenchman for a drink?"

"He's not *my* anything. And no, I am not meeting him anywhere."

"Why?" the younger woman puzzled. "Did you have a fight with him, too?"

"No, of course not. I'm just ready to call it a day. We were on the road early this morning."

"Better watch out, honey. Someone else might snag that hunk."

"Why would I worry about that? There's nothing between Etienne and me. I'm a married woman."

"But your husband isn't here. You know what they say, 'While the cat's away…'"

Sylvia shook her head. "Not interested."

"If you say so." Deanna dismissed the denial. She turned back to the mirror to fluff her hair then glanced over at Sylvia. "If you're sure you're not interested…maybe I'll make a play for Mr. Tall-Dark-and-Sexy."

"Be my guest. I'm going to just curl up in this cozy bed and see what's on TV."

Chapter Twenty-Seven

"Fine. Call me when you get near town so I'll know when to pick you up."

Dave set down the phone. He'd forced himself to hang up before he made a jerk of himself and begged Sylvie not to do anything that would jeopardize their marriage. The last couple of months had strained their relationship so much he was certain one more tug would cause it to break like an overstretched rubber band.

Then what would he do?

Syl and the kids had been his whole life. Everything he'd become or accomplished had been for them. She owned his heart from almost the moment they'd met in high school. God blessed him by sending Sylvia his way again years later. For the last twenty-six years, he had been the luckiest man in the world to be Sylvia's husband.

Had those years together been a sham? Had Sylvia been biding her time until someone richer, younger, better looking came along?

A few months ago, if someone had hinted at such a notion, Dave would have laughed out loud. He loved Sylvia, and she loved him. Sure, they'd had occasional spats—what married couple hadn't?—but they had built a good life together, a life based on love, respect, and trust. They enjoyed spending time together and doing things together.

Except lately. Now, Sylvie was off doing things with other people. Other *men!*

Because you were too stubborn to go with her, his conscience reminded him.

Dave brushed aside the thought, knowing it was true but not wanting to dwell on what he might have done to their relationship. He trusted her. He really did. Sylvia was too honorable to be unfaithful to him. Still, his stubbornness had damaged their marriage, and he wasn't sure how to fix it. He couldn't abandon his values, but he also knew he couldn't bear to lose Sylvia either.

Instead, he went into his office, intending to drown himself in work. If Sylvia wasn't coming home until morning, he would stay so busy he wouldn't have time to think. He settled in his desk chair, intending to turn on his PC, but stopped at the sight of his mother's fancy, lace-trimmed journal sitting on the corner of the desk where he'd put it that afternoon.

He picked up the heavy book and studied the well-worn cover. Should he read it? He certainly had enough time, and Muriel had told him it was important. He shrugged. Maybe a walk down Memory Lane would occupy his mind and keep him from fretting about Sylvia. It was either that or get rip-roaring drunk.

Choosing the journal, he carried it into the den, switched on the pole lamp beside his recliner then made himself comfortable. The satin closure on the book was brittle with age and beginning to shred. Dave carefully untied the bow, trying not to do any further damage to the ribbon. He opened the book then squinted at the tiny, flowing script covering the pages. *Time to get new glasses,* he thought. He dug a pair of readers from the pocket of his armchair caddy, put them on, and began on the first page.

The first entry was dated May 1, 1943. *Two years before Mure was born,* he thought. He recalled hearing that his parents had met about then. He focused on the words.

Today is May Day. I'm excited about going to the May Day Dance. Daddy wouldn't let me buy a new dress. He said it was a frivolous waste. Of course, Mom wouldn't contradict him. She told me I'd just have to wear one of my old gowns. Instead, I borrowed one from my friend Suzy Willis. It's so pretty with a full, white georgette skirt and a red bodice with a lovely sweetheart neckline. Suzy only wore it once—for her older sister's wedding—and it doesn't fit her anymore, so she's letting me wear it for the dance. Mom said the dress would really be more suitable for Valentine's Day than a May Day dance, but I don't care. I love it! It makes me feel so beautiful. I just know something wonderful is going to happen tonight.

The next entry was written the following day and was filled with more girlie talk about what her friends wore to the dance and how the hall was decorated. Dave almost skipped it until he spotted his father's name at the bottom of the page.

I met the most wonderful boy at the dance—a man really, since he's nearly five years older than me. His name is William Miller, and he goes to Michigan State with the Alt boys. He and his parents moved here from England just before the war broke out, so Liam—that's what his friends call him—has an absolutely dreamy accent. He said he'd noticed me as soon as I walked into the dance, because red is his favorite color. We talked and danced almost the whole night, and he said he'd call on me later this week and maybe we can go get a soda. I'll have to see if I can borrow my friend Mary's red cardigan. Oh, I just knew this dress was magical.

Dave smiled. His mother sounded almost like Lynne had when she was a teenager. He remembered driving his daughter and her friends to dances and listening to them squeal and giggle over the all the cute boys they'd danced with.

He flipped through the pages, reading random passages and seeing how his parents' relationship had continued and progressed. Over the next eighteen months, they'd moved from a few stolen kisses to descriptions of steamier encounters that made him feel uncomfortably like a Peeping Tom. He skipped past most of those then stopped at an entry dated two years later and decorated with doodles of lovers' hearts.

I am so excited. Liam is picking me up in a little while to go out to eat. He said to wear his favorite red dress, because he's taking me somewhere special. He's going to ask me to marry him. I just know he is. And I'm going to say yes. I'm going to be his wife, and I'm going to love him, and we will have the very best life. I am not going to worry about what Father will say. He won't approve, I know it, because Liam doesn't have a good job. He does, really, but teaching elementary school is not a career that's going to make a lot of money. But Liam says he doesn't care, because he'll have the summers off and lots of holidays. So I don't care what Father thinks. Liam and I are going to be so happy together. I'll be a good wife, prudent enough to put away a few dollars each week. But we won't worry about every single penny we spend or about how many coats of wax I put on the dining room table. And I have a surprise for Liam. We're going to have a baby next spring. I'll tell him tonight. I can hardly wait.

So Grandfather Beaumont didn't approve of his dad. Dave snorted. That was no surprise. Grandfather hadn't approved of much of anything. Dave imagined his grandfather had nearly burst a blood vessel when he'd found out his daughter was pregnant months before her wedding. Still, none of this explained why Muriel felt it was so necessary to read the journal.

Dave turned the page and read the next day's entry.

I was right. Liam asked me to marry him after dinner last night. Of course, I said yes. He bought me the loveliest engagement ring, although he said the stone is way too small and promised to replace it with a larger one by our five-year anniversary. I told him the ring is absolutely perfect just the way it is…and it is! I've never owned a ring before—not even a class ring from my high school. Father says jewelry is a frivolous waste. I used my own money from babysitting jobs to buy the few pairs of earrings I have.

Liam is as excited as I am about the baby; however, unlike me—I want to shout it from the roof I'm so happy—he wants to keep it a secret. He knows his parents will be elated but is worried about how mine will react. To be honest, I'm worried about that, too. Daddy can be so hateful sometimes and say such hurtful things. However, we're both of age, so I've agreed to meet him this afternoon when he finishes teaching, and we'll go to the courthouse to get our marriage license. We plan to slip away early on Friday and get married by a Justice of the Peace. Liam will make all the arrangements. He says I'm not to worry about a thing. My goodness, what will I wear?

Dave smiled. His mother's excitement filled the page. She reminded him of Sylvia, who'd also blossomed despite her confining home life. He wished they could have met. He knew they would have loved one another. He wished so many things. With a sigh for what might have been, he turned the page and continued reading.

His father had been right to worry. Grandpa Beaumont had been livid when he discovered his only child had eloped. He stopped just short of disowning her. Surprisingly, his grandmother's main concern seemed to be where they planned to live. She offered to come over and help clean.

Several pages later, water spots blurred the ink, and Dave realized his mother must have been crying as she'd written the entry. He began reading to see what had upset her.

What a horrible night. We invited Mom and Dad to dinner since I'm beginning to show, so we needed to tell them about the baby. I was so excited. I cleaned all day then cooked a special dinner—beef roast with potatoes and carrots—and I made Dad's favorite coconut layer cake for dessert. I thought he'd be pleased to see I'd made everything from scratch. Instead, he complained about how much the roast must have cost. He said I should have made a meatloaf! I could tell Liam wanted to tell him to mind his own business, but he held his tongue.

After I served dessert, we told them our happy news. I thought they'd be happy to have a grandchild on the way. Instead, Daddy ranted and yelled. He accused us of being reckless and irresponsible for "having a baby when you can barely afford a mortgage payment." That's so unfair. We pay our bills and even manage to put aside a tidy amount each month. Mother's reaction was worse in its own way. I started to cry when all she had to say to us was "Babies are messy and cause too much work. Please don't expect me to come over here to clean up after them."

That did it as far as Liam was concerned. He got their coats and calmly asked them to leave our house, but I could tell he was furious. I was proud of him for standing up to Father and being protective of me. But I do love Father, despite his temper, and I worry how this will affect our relationship.

After that, most of the entries related every day scenes: family celebrations, visits from Liam's family, outings with their friends. There were two entries when Muriel was born. The first was the joyous raving of a new mother; the other a somewhat sad account of her parents' refusal to visit and meet their granddaughter.

Three years later, she wrote:

Our family is so perfect. We have a little girl and a little boy now. Liam is a good father and a good provider. Last week, we had an agent come to the house and talk to us about life insurance. We took out policies so the house will be paid for and the children provided for if anything should happen to us. I really don't like to think about such things, but Liam insisted. He's always so practical and concerned about all of us. He's right of course, and I'm so lucky to have him in my life.

Dave frowned. His mother's words completely contradicted the impression his grandfather had painted. According to her, his father hadn't been an impractical spendthrift at all. In fact, it sounded like he'd planned ahead and cared deeply for his family's future.

Dave turned the pages and soon found the first entry about himself:

I can't believe it. After eight years, I'm expecting again. Liam will be so excited. He always said he wanted a houseful of children, and now we'll have three. I wonder if this one will be a boy or a girl? Will the baby be as serious as our little Muriel or be a cut-up like Billy? Oh, I can't wait to tell Liam. He'll be over the moon with happiness. So am I!

He smiled at his mother's happiness, could almost feel her love pouring from the pages. He'd forgotten how much he had loved being around her, playing at her feet with his toy cars while she sewed or curling up beside her for a bedtime story. He turned the page, eager to remember more.

The children are growing so fast. I want to show them so much. I think they love to travel nearly as much as their parents do. I love showing them new things, taking them to the places I'd always wanted to visit. There's so much to see in our wonderful state! Liam and I do it without spending a lot of money. We camp on the beaches of Lake Michigan, stroll through the tulips at the Holland Tulip Festival, and dance our way through the Highland Festival up north. When the children are a little older, we'll take them to the capitol in Lansing and to watch cars being made in Detroit. Father was so wrong. It's never a waste of money to visit new places and experience new cultures. It is so important for my children to understand that. There is so much to see in this wonderful world of ours.

Dave stilled at the last sentence. He could almost hear his mother's quiet, musical voice talking to him. "Davey, there's so much to see in this wonderful world of ours. I want to show you everything. Look! See how beautiful the sand is here? And feel how silky it is on your little bare feet? Scoop up a handful of it, honey. Do you see how it's made of millions of little stones in so many different colors? And look at all the little animals in the water."

He remembered how she'd taken him by the hand and

led him into the water, pointing out all the creatures there, while cautioning him not to go any deeper than his knees without someone older to watch him.

With that memory came a flood of wonderful recollections of his father as well. He remembered riding on his dad's shoulders on Memorial Day and the Fourth of July, so he could see the parade over the heads of the crowd. His father would bounce him up and down in time with the music, making him laugh with pleasure. Afterward, they picnicked in the park with Mom's delicious potato salad and fried chicken. At night, they'd watch the colorful fireworks show. His father had loved the ones that whistled as they climbed into the heavens; his mother preferred the ones that exploded in the sky like giant orange chrysanthemums.

The family had had such fun making day trips in their big old Chevy. Muriel and Billy would read the Burma Shave signs posted along the highway. They'd all sing silly songs and play License Plate Bingo or I Spy. They'd made hundreds of happy memories together. Memories he'd forgotten or suppressed once he moved into his grandfather's gloomy house.

Eager to learn more about life with his parents, Dave continued reading. He was grateful his mother had taken the time to write down her thoughts to preserve these precious glimpses of his past. Thanks to her journal, Dave saw his parents as they really were, not colored by his Grandfather's festering bitterness.

His mother seldom mentioned her parents in the journal. When she did, it was with a tolerance that again reminded Dave of Sylvia. Instead of dwelling on sad things, his mother had filled the pages of her journal with love and happiness. She wrote about his father's success as an educator and his promotion to principal. She was very proud of him but expressed a bit of concern when he wanted to take flying lessons. Still, she'd been there to wave and cheer when he'd made his first solo flight, and had even begun to get on board with the idea of flying the family to other states for vacations.

Before he knew it, Dave reached the last diary entry. His mother's handwriting was a little different now from the flowing schoolgirl loops and flourishes that had started the journal. Now, her letters were neat and compact with only an occasional flourish when she was particularly happy or excited.

Liam and I leave tomorrow for his conference in California. I wasn't too keen on leaving the children, but he says it will be a romantic getaway for the two of us, a chance to "reconnect" as a couple. Mrs. McHenry, our housekeeper, will stay at the house with the kids while we're gone. Liam has borrowed a plane from one of his pals at the airport, so it won't cost us much more than if he'd gone alone.

Dave set down the book and frowned at the page. His father had *borrowed* a plane? Where was the extravagant purchase Grandpa Beaumont had brought up every time Dave had wanted to spend a few dollars of the money he'd earned on his newspaper route? *You're just like your father, throwing away money on foolishness. I suppose the next thing you'll want is a blasted airplane.* Dave shook his head. Obviously, the plane was another of his grandfather's fabrications. He picked up the book again and continued to read.

I'll miss the kids and would love to bring them along. But neither of us wants them to miss school. Still, we're a family, and I hate to leave them behind. They'd learn so much about our country, seeing it from the air. They're only children for such a short time. I can't believe Muriel is already starting her second year in college, and Billy will be graduating high school in June. The way the years fly by, it won't be long before they'll be married themselves. Of course, then I'll have grandbabies to cuddle and spoil. Won't that be something?

Even our little Davy has grown so much over the past summer. He's so much like his father: intelligent, prudent, kind, and devilishly handsome. He's inherited Liam's artistic eye, too. They spend hours together, carving all sorts of whimsical animals from scraps of wood or plotting out designs for the flower gardens. I think I'll miss him the most.

Dave leaned back and closed his eyes.

Oh, Mom, I miss you, too.

Chapter Twenty-Eight

Etienne sat at the hotel bar, barely listening to the man, Jerry something or another, who the tour director had assigned as a roommate. He couldn't remember the last time he'd shared a room with anyone other than his wife, Elise, or some other female companion. Certainly not since boarding school, he decided. He hadn't shared any more willingly back then than he did now. Unfortunately, tonight, he had no choice. Etienne tried to make other arrangements, even offered a bribe to the desk clerk, but the blizzard had stranded too many people, busloads of concert-goers as well as diners in the restaurant. Every room was filled. Etienne didn't mind spending the night, but he certainly would have picked a different roommate.

Perhaps one with glossy black hair and mischievous blue eyes, he thought as he nursed a glass of very poor quality Piesporter.

"Is this seat taken?"

He turned at the sultry female voice, hoping Sylvia had decided to accept his offer of nightcaps after all. Instead, her roommate Deanna stood by his elbow, batting long, mascara-caked eyelashes in his direction. Her long hair tumbled over her shoulders in a riot of dark curls, almost hiding the Traveling Solo logo on the too-tight, hot pink polo she wore.

Before Etienne could answer, Jerry leaped up and motioned to his barstool. "Here, take my seat. I'll move down one so you can be between us."

"I don't want to interrupt or anything," she said, but her body language, as she leaned in and accidentally brushed her chest against Etienne's arm, said something far different.

He smiled but turned on his chair to look back at the bar entrance, effectively easing away from the woman. "Sylvia, she is coming down to join you, *non*?"

"Nope. Said bars and casinos aren't her thing. So I'm here all by my lonely self," she said, leaning toward him again.

"Well, we can't have that, can we?" Jerry said with a laugh that reminded Etienne of the guy selling automobiles on the television. And, just like the man on the television, his roommate was trying a bit too hard. "What can I get you to drink?"

But Deanna didn't seem to mind. She shifted her seat to face his direction. Pointing to his glass, she playfully asked, "What are you having? I'll have the same."

Etienne listened as the pair continued to chat, smiling at their clumsy flirtation and trying to figure out how he could turn things to his advantage. His opportunity came when Jerry excused himself to use the men's room.

"You strike me as a very smart lady, *cherie*," Etienne said, giving the curvy brunette his biggest, toothpaste ad smile. "One who would appreciate a good opportunity when eet came along."

"I do?"

"You do, indeed, *cherie*," he replied then took a sip of his wine. "One who might like to make an easy thousand dollars, *non*?"

"A thousand dollars?" she echoed. She gave him a lazy

smile and draped her arm over his shoulder. "And just what would I have to do to earn so much money tonight?"

Etienne reached up and patted the hand resting on his shoulder. "Nothing illegal, *ma petite*. I give you my word on that."

****

Sylvia still couldn't believe Dave had disconnected on her. He'd disconnected without even telling her goodbye. She wanted to call him back and ask what was up with that, but she already knew. She'd tried to be supportive of Dave's decision to continue working. She'd even had a nice family party to celebrate his promotion, but their marriage was mired in trouble, and she had no idea how to fix it. Over the last few weeks, the tension gnawed at them both.

"I love you, David Miller," she whispered to the empty room and blinked back the tears that threatened to overflow. "And I miss you. I miss *us*."

She'd been glad when her man-crazy roommate had decided to go down to the bar to see what might be going on down there. Deanna's chatter had scraped on Sylvia's raw nerves, but now, the room felt too quiet. She considered going downstairs, too, but quickly dismissed the idea. Bars and such weren't really her thing. Besides, in her mood, she'd feel just as alone in a roomful of people. Maybe there was something on TV. A sitcom would suit her nicely. She'd take a quick shower then climb into bed and see what was playing.

It'll be just my luck that all the channels will be running tear-jerker romances tonight, she thought as she grabbed one of the complimentary robes from the hotel and headed for the bathroom.

A half hour later, Sylvia was propped up in bed, flipping through a quilting magazine from her tote bag and half watching some mindless, primetime game show on the television. The hot shower had eased some of the tension from her travel-weary muscles but had done little to relax her mind. She really missed Dave. The old Dave. The one with the corny jokes and the gentle ways. When had he changed? Or had she been the one who'd changed?

She retrieved her purse from the dresser and hunted through it. In the bottom of the purse, half hidden by discarded tissues and a cosmetic bag that held pens and aspirins as well as make-up these days, she found the small, suede pouch she wanted. She untied the drawstrings then shook out the contents.

The wooden heart, carved to resemble the design on the Calico Heart quilt, nestled in her palm. Some of the carving had faded, but the piece was still gorgeous in her eyes. Dave had carved it for her and for more than twenty-six years, she'd either worn or carried it. A symbol of Dave's love. Now, she fingered the broken bale and wondered if it, too, was symbolic of their marriage. Broken.

A sound at the door startled her from her reverie. She'd thrown the night latch when Deanna had gone downstairs, and now her roommate wouldn't be able to open the door. Sylvia hurried to release the lock then threw open the door, an apology ready on her lips.

An apology that died when she saw the man standing in the hallway, holding a key to her room in his hand.

"Etienne!" she gasped, clutching the neckline of her robe more firmly closed. "What on earth are you doing here?"

"*Bonsoir*," he greeted then held up a wine bottle and two glasses. "Since you did not want to go down to the bar with me for a nightcap, I bring the nightcap to you."

"That's very thoughtful of you, Etienne," Sylvia replied, standing so the door was between them. "I'm sure it's a very nice wine. But I'm afraid I can't let you come into my room."

"And why is that, *cherie*?"

"It wouldn't be proper, Etienne. I'm a married woman."

"So you have said. But why would such a thing matter? You have—how do you say eet?—an open marriage, *non*?"

"An open—No! Of course I don't. What would make you think such a thing?"

"Do not be embarrassed, *cherie*. Eet is quite acceptable in my country! Since you travel alone, and you rarely speak of your husband, I assumed eet was also acceptable in your country. Such an arrangement does not mean you are not fond of your spouse. I am quite fond of Elise."

Her anger at his audacity nearly overtook the shock she'd felt when she'd found him at her door. "I travel without Dave because he doesn't like to travel. I'm not *fond* of him; I *love* him. And I certainly don't have an *open marriage*."

"Sylvia, *cherie*, please forgive me. I was wrong to assume you no longer had feelings for your husband. I will not make that mistake again," he apologized. He took a step forward, giving her a charming smile. "Let me come inside, and we will have a few drinks and you—"

"No! Capital N, capital O!" Sylvia declared. "How dare you come to my room and proposition me like some common tramp?"

"*Cherie*, eet is not like that, I assure you," he said raising his hands. "I respect and admire you, I enjoy your company and—"

"Wait a minute!" she interrupted. "Who on earth is Elise?"

"What?"

"A minute ago, you said you were 'quite fond of Elise.' Who—" She paused as the realization hit her. "Good grief, Etienne! You're not a widower, are you?"

"Please, you misunderstand things—" he said, raising his hands that still held the wine and glasses.

"Oh, no, I understand things quite well, mister," she shot back. She pointed to the key card he held in the same hand as the wine bottle. "When I came to undo the latch, you already had my door unlocked! Where did you get a key to my room?"

He shrugged. "That is not important, *cherie*—"

"Maybe not to you, but it's rather important to me." She held out her hand, palm up. "Give it here."

"But where will I sleep?"

If she'd thought she'd been angry at his audacity before, now she was livid. "That is no concern of mine. However..."

She paused and held out her hand again. "If you don't give me that key by the time I count to three, I'm going to scream bloody murder. Then I'm sure the local police will find a very nice jail cell for you to sleep in. They don't appreciate men breaking into women's hotel rooms in *my* country."

Chapter Twenty-Nine

"Hey, boss, how about lunch?"

"What?" Dave looked up from the spreadsheet he'd been studying to find his secretary, Shelly, bundled in her winter coat and standing in the office doorway.

"Lunch. It's the meal between breakfast and supper. Not that you'd notice since you always have your nose buried in work when we go down to the cafeteria."

He patted his stomach. "This spare tire tells me I couldn't have missed very many lunches..."

"Too many," she scolded with the familiarity that came after years of working together. "Besides, they're featuring Reubens today in the sub shop, and I know you like those. Grab your coat and join us. Unless Mr. Vice-President thinks he's too good to hang out with us lowly worker bees."

"You're right." He gestured around his crowded, temporary office. Cardboard file boxes of client records covered nearly the entire floor. More were stacked on the side chairs. January was always a crazy month as clients closed their books and tax time approached. "I need to escape before this luxurious office goes to my head. Besides, a Reuben sounds delicious."

The downtown sub shop was only a block away from the Davis Andrews building, but frigid January wind whipped down the sidewalk, making the distance seem longer. The scent of freshly baked bread welcomed them when they opened the restaurant door, and Dave was glad he'd decided to come along. They joined a table of their coworkers just as a busy waitress approached to take their orders. It was an easy one, Reubens and coffee for everyone.

"Can you believe Valentine's Day is just around the corner?" Shelly asked. "What are you guys getting your wives?"

One of the men groaned. "I don't know. Marcie tells me I never think about her when I buy her gifts. I don't know what she means. I think about her all the time. Especially the way she's been acting since Christmas."

"Uh-oh, Ken, what did you do to upset her?" Shelly asked.

He shrugged. "We remodeled the kitchen before Thanksgiving, and she got all upset because I told her the new appliances were her Christmas present. They cost a lot of money, but we got exactly the ones she wanted. Was I supposed to buy her a present on top of that?"

Dave winced. He knew what Sylvia would say if he had tried to count an appliance as a gift.

"Maybe she figured the remodeling was as much for you as for her," a younger guy by the name of Brandon suggested.

"Sure it was," Ken agreed. "Just like the fishing rod she bought me for my last birthday benefitted her as well as me. I bring home plenty of nice fish for our dinners all summer."

"I don't know, my girlfriend has a rule about not giving her anything with a cord as a gift. I think household appliances fall into the same category."

Dave had to agree, but he decided not to argue and upset Ken further. Besides, all this conversation made him wonder what to do for Sylvia this Valentine's Day. Things had been pretty strained between them since she came back from her trip. He wanted to tell her about his mother's journal, maybe read parts of it together with her. With Muriel's permission, Dave had scanned the journal, making copies for himself and his brother before returning the original to his sister. Most of all, Dave wanted to apologize to Sylvia for putting his grandfather's warped values before his wife's dreams and wishes. He had so much to share, but fear held him back.

What if Sylvie no longer wanted to do things with him? What if she wanted to leave him because she no longer loved him and was attracted to the Frenchman or someone else? Dave didn't know what he'd do then. Sylvia meant everything to him.

He remembered when they were first married and did everything together. Somehow, he needed to reconnect with her in the same way. He remembered their first Valentine's Day together. Sylvia had used scrap fabric and made quilted Valentine gifts for everyone. An eyeglass case for him and a lap blanket for his grandfather. Grandpa Beaumont had actually smiled at the gift and said, "You chose a smart girl, David. She doesn't waste money on things we can't use."

Knowing his wife had his grandfather's approval had meant a lot to him, since he'd always tried to please the older man and live up to his expectations. Now, Dave realized just how misguided he had been, but he wouldn't allow himself to become embittered. Valentine's Day was about love, and he planned to win back the woman whose heart he had almost trampled.

He remembered the gift he had once carved for her from an old piece of oak. It was a small heart, carved with a design she'd admired at a quilt show. He'd made a loop at the top so it could hang on a necklace. He'd finished it by carving their initials on the back. Then he'd stained and polished it until it had gleamed.

He'd almost been embarrassed to give her such a simple gift, but he'd put a note in with it saying that she would always have his heart. She'd claimed it was the best gift she'd ever received and had worn it every day for several years. He'd intended to make her a matching jewelry box, but life had gotten busy. He hadn't carved in years. Once the kids had come along, it had seemed like there just was never enough time.

But now, the kids were grown and gone. Sure, he was busy with his promotion, but he had time when Syl went to her quilt group. Maybe he'd try his hand at carving again. He could stop at the lumberyard on his way home and look for a nice piece of oak. He could keep it in the trunk until Syl went to bed then sneak it into his workshop in the basement. If he carved her another gift, could he win back her heart? Or would her loving heart be lost to him after he'd nearly tossed it aside?

It was definitely worth a try.

Chapter Thirty

"Is everything alright, dear?"

Sylvia looked up from the quilt book she was perusing to find Lila standing on the other side of the pattern counter, studying her. Concern etched the older woman's gentle features.

"You've been quiet all evening."

"I'm fine," Sylvia replied, trying to muster a reassuring smile, but tears brimmed to the surface betraying her.

"Are you worried about Myra's announcement? Were you surprised?" her friend asked, referring to the card they'd found on the store bulletin board where the Stitching Post's owner usually hung free quilt patterns and her monthly newsletter. Tonight, Myra had posted a short notice that she and her husband were planning to sell the quilt shop and retire somewhere warmer than snowy Michigan.

Sylvia nodded, although it hadn't really been a complete surprise. In the twenty-odd years Sylvia had been coming to the shop, Myra had always talked about retiring to Florida or Arizona one day. Still, the announcement had hit Sylvia hard, reminding her of how much her own life had changed over the last eight months. Now, she blinked, forcing back her tears.

Lila reached over the high counter and gave Sylvia's hand a motherly squeeze. "Don't worry, sweetie. Myra told me she listed the shop with Theresa. You know our Tee. She'll find the perfect new owner for us. Someone who loves quilting as much as we do."

"I hope so. I've made so many friends here. I'd hate to lose all of you."

"Don't be silly," the older woman paused and scooted a tall stool over to the counter. She perched on it, leaned her elbows on the counter, and settled in for a chat. "Honey, even if this place closes—and there's no reason to think it will—we'll find somewhere else to get together. At a church or in someone's home. And we'll all still be friends."

"Probably. But it won't be the same."

"Of course it won't. Our lives are full of changes. Sickness, health, births, deaths, marriages, divorces—"

Hearing the D word made Sylvia's heart lurch. Her hands trembled, and she moved them quickly to her lap, hoping her friend hadn't noticed. But Lila's face told Sylvia that she had.

"I'm sure you're right," Sylvia rushed to reassure her.

"Now, why doesn't that convince me?" Lila asked, cupping her chin in her hands. "What's really going on, Sylvia Miller? I noticed you haven't worked on your travel quilt—or much of anything—since before Christmas. 'Fess up, honey. Tell Mama Lila what's really bothering you."

"It's nothing." Sylvia puffed out a breath. "At least I hope it isn't."

"That doesn't sound like *nothing* to me," her friend remarked and studied her over the top of her wire-framed glasses.

"I don't want to bother you with my problems."

"Nonsense. We're friends, it's what friends do! Is everything okay at home?"

Sylvia glanced at the corner where their other friends were chatting over their needlework. No one seemed to have noticed Lila and her having their little heart-to-heart. Still, she lowered her voice so the others couldn't hear before continuing. "Nothing is okay, Lila."

"Oh, honey. I'm so sorry. What happened?"

"Everything and nothing," Sylvia replied. She took a deep breath. "Remember I told you Dave changed his mind about retiring early and said he doesn't want to travel?"

Lila nodded. "He had the chance to become vice-president at his company. I thought you agreed with his decision."

"He really never asked. But I still tried to be as supportive as possible. I thought getting that promotion would make him happy, and it's only for a few more years, after all. But things have only gotten worse. And since I started traveling without him, all we ever do is argue."

"Maybe his new position is the culprit. He's probably put a lot of pressure on himself to succeed."

"I could understand if that were the case. But Dave comes home late, barely says a word while he eats dinner, then closets himself in his office or the basement. Most nights, he doesn't come to bed until after I'm asleep. Sometimes, he doesn't come to bed at all. He's slept more than once in his office chair."

"Have you tried to talk to him? Ask what's bothering him?"

"I finally decided to do just that last night. I went to his office to talk to him and…"

"What happened?" Lila asked.

Sylvia choked back the lump that had had formed in her throat and took a shuddering breath.

"I was in the hallway outside his office, about to knock on the door, when I heard him on the phone. I think he was talking to our attorney, Jim Anderson. Dave said something about going into the office this morning to sign some papers…Lila…I think my husband is planning to divorce me."

Chapter Thirty-One

"And we want to wish all our radio listeners a very Happy Valentine's Day on this bright—"

"Oh please, stop already," Sylvia whispered and jabbed the power button on the kitchen radio to shut it off.

She didn't need any more reminders of what today was. For the last two weeks, it was all she heard when she turned on the radio or TV, all she saw in magazines and store ads. All those hearts and flowers and happy couples had brought tears to her eyes every time, no matter how much she'd tried to steel herself against them. Now, here it was: the big day itself.

In the silent kitchen, she reached in her jeans pocket and brought out the worn wooden heart that Dave had given her on Valentine's Day so long ago. She ran her fingertip over the lovingly carved lines, smiled when she encountered the tooth mark on the back from the day little Davey had decided to use it as a teething ring. She remembered how Dave had offered to sand off the mark, but they'd decided to leave it as a souvenir. They'd been so happy and crazy in love.

She bit her bottom lip to keep away the tears that threatened to overwhelm her at the memory. The last few weeks had stretched her nerves to the limit. When Dave left each morning, she worried he would come home that night to tell her he was divorcing her. Instead, more often than not, he came home and they ate in silence and spent the evening in separate parts of the house. She didn't know how much longer she could stand this agonizing waiting.

Today would be the worst day of all.

"Pull yourself together, Sylvia," she chided herself. "Stop thinking and just get breakfast going. You can cry after Dave leaves for work."

As she opened the cupboard to get out plates and coffee mugs, she spotted the Valentine card she'd bought for Dave weeks ago and had tucked in the corner for safekeeping. Hearing his footsteps in the hallway, she started to close the cupboard and just leave the card there. Instead, she grabbed it and slapped it down on the breakfast table beside Dave's coffee mug. If he read it fine; if not...

Well, she could cry about that later, too.

"Morning," Dave mumbled, coming into the kitchen.

Sylvia was surprised to see him still in pajamas instead of his suit. Oh no, he must have planned to eat before dressing, and her daydreaming had distracted her. Nothing was ready. She hurried to the refrigerator trying to decide what would be the quickest breakfast to fix. "Let me get eggs and bacon going, and I'll get you a cup of coffee."

"I don't feel like eggs and bacon."

"What?" Sylvia frowned and turned to look at him.

"I don't want eggs and bacon. I think I want waffles this morning," he said, sitting down at the table and stretching his legs in front of him.

Sylvia held her breath, wondering if he'd notice her card. However he didn't so much as glance at the card. Instead, he spun the chair around and straddled it. Crossing his arms on the chair back, he rested his chin on them the way he always had when they were dating. Back then, she'd thought he looked cute and sexy at the same time. She bit the inside of her lip. He still looked that way to her.

"Yeah," he said, nodding his head. "I definitely have a taste for waffles."

"Dave, I haven't made waffles in ages. The batter will take forever, and I'm not even sure where the waffle iron is," she protested.

Her husband shrugged. "It's probably still wherever you put it when you used it last."

"I suppose." Confused at such odd behavior on a workday, she went to the closet where she stored her kitchen gadgets that weren't used very frequently. "I think I put it in here."

"Let me give you a hand," Dave offered, getting up from the table. "You might have put it on the top shelf and won't be able to reach it."

She nodded then opened the pantry door.

A gasp escaped her lips. Sitting smack in the middle of the shelf where her mixer and bread machine should have been was a large package carefully wrapped in shiny red paper and finished with an elaborate, white satin bow.

"What's that?" she asked.

"Looks like a present," Dave said. He reached past her and picked up the package. He checked the tag on top then held the box out to her. "It says it's for you."

Puzzled, Sylvia took the package and carried it to the counter. It was only a little larger than a shoebox but seemed exceptionally heavy for its size. She frowned. "I don't understand. Did one of the kids—"

Dave shook his head. "Just open it."

She nodded then began to carefully peel off the wrapping paper. Dave laughed and grabbed a corner of the paper and gave it a tug, tearing it loose.

"Dave!" *What had gotten into him this morning?*

"It's only paper, Sylvie. Go ahead and tear into it."

She shrugged and pulled the paper free to reveal a plain cardboard box sealed with several layers of packing tape. Using the steak knife Dave handed her from the knife block on the counter, she slit the tape then lifted the flaps. Inside, layers of heart-imprinted tissue covered the object inside.

"Here, let me hold the box for you."

He lifted the box from the counter and held it out so she could more easily reach inside it. For a moment, his eyes met hers over the box, and he looked so much like the boy she'd married, it brought tears to her eyes again. Ducking her head to hide them from Dave, she lifted the object from the box. It was square and hard and surprisingly heavy. *Surely divorce papers don't come in a box this big.*

Taking a deep breath, she tore away the tissue covering and found a beautiful, handmade jewelry box with a replica of the Calico Heart carved on its lid. Her hand flew to her mouth and happy tears spilled from her eyes. "Oh, David."

"Happy Valentine's Day, Sylvie." Dave grinned, boyishly. "Do you like it?"

"Like it?" she whispered, running her fingers over the carved top. "I love it! It matches my heart."

"I always promised I'd make one for you. But I hadn't seen you wear the heart for years—"

"The bale broke, so I couldn't wear it anymore. But..." She paused and pulled the heart from her pocket. "I always keep it with me. Either in my pocket or my purse."

"I didn't know. I hadn't seen it for a while, so I wasn't sure if you still liked the design or if you'd still want it on a jewelry box. It took a lot longer to finish than I thought. That's why I was locked up in my workshop so late the last week." He grabbed a napkin and patted at her wet cheeks.

"Are you okay, honey? If you don't like it, you can just tell me. I know I'm kind of out of practice..."

"Oh, David, it's the best gift I've ever received," she assured him.

"Oh." He frowned and seemed to consider her words. "Then you probably don't want to look inside."

She froze. "What do you mean?"

"Well, if this is the best gift ever..." He paused and winked. "Maybe you should just open it, honey."

With shaking hands, Sylvia set the beautiful jewelry box on the counter then lifted the lid. The smell of newly sanded wood filled her nostrils. For some reason, she'd always associated that scent with her handyman husband. She gave him a smile then peeked inside the box. The smile froze on her lips.

A legal-sized envelope lay in the bottom of the box. An envelope with the name of their attorney, Jim Anderson, imprinted in the corner and her name carefully handwritten across the front. *Oh no. Surely Dave wouldn't be so cruel as to serve her with divorce papers this way?*

"What-what is it?"

"Open it and find out, Sylvie."

With her heart thudding, she picked up the envelope and lifted the flap. Her hands shook so hard she could barely remove the contents, a single sheet of paper with a photo of a large motor home stapled to it. Puzzled, Sylvia looked at paper and saw it was a bill of sale for the vehicle and made out to her.

"I bought it for you," Dave said, giving her a tenuous smile. "For us, actually. Jim took care of the title work for me. I was worried we wouldn't get it in time. We almost didn't. I just went in and signed the papers last night after work."

He took her hand and brought them to his lips. "Now that I've been promoted I know I can't get away for long trips except on vacations...but we could take weekend getaways, couldn't we, Sylvie? That is if you still want me to go with you. I wouldn't blame you if you didn't. I know I've been a stupid fool...Can you ever forgive me?"

"David Miller, I love you!" Sylvia exclaimed, throwing

her arms around his neck.

"I'll take that as a yes," he said as he pulled her close and kissed her.

"Definitely a yes," she whispered then gave him another longer, deeper kiss. "I might just have to show you how much this evening."

"Why not now?" He grinned. "After all, I'm still in my pajamas."

"Dave, you'll be late for work!" Her protest turned to giggles as he slipped his hand under the hem of her t-shirt.

"I took the day off," he murmured against her lips. "It's Valentine's Day, and I still remember a much better way to spend it than going to the office."

Chapter Thirty-Two

"Bye, Mom! Bye, Dad! Love you!"

"Uh, oh, your mom's about to cry." Ron laughed, putting his arms around Lynne's waist as they stood to see her parents off.

"Of course she is," his wife replied, leaning back against his chest. "She's happy."

John watched as his father helped his mother into the passenger seat of the older but still luxurious RV before getting into the driver's seat. His sister was right; they did look happy. He turned to the others gathered in the driveway of his parents' home—his brother D2, Lynne and Ron, his mother's friends Ellen, Sue, Lila, and several others from their quilt group, too. In a voice loud enough for his mother to hear in the RV, he declared, "Mom always cries."

"Yep," his brother added just as loudly. "Happy or sad, she always cries."

"I do not!" Sylvia called back at them. But, as she waved to the family and good friends who'd come to see her and Dave off on their trip, her eyes filled with happy tears. "Well, okay," she conceded. "Maybe I do."

"I guess I'll have to put a few more bucks into that mascara budget," Dave teased, reaching across the front console to squeeze Sylvia's hand.

"I guess you will, Mr. Vice-President," she replied as he maneuvered the big motor home into the street then switched on the portable GPS. He looked so relaxed and happy behind the wheel. Almost as happy as she felt.

"You know, Sylvie, I really appreciate your support about this promotion. Thank you for being so understanding."

"Of course, I understand, honey. You told me it's what you've always wanted but never thought you could do. Just like I always dreamed of traveling."

"Still, I want you to know how much it means to me. I know you had your heart set on us both retiring."

"And we still will...just not together...not yet."

"Are you sure you don't mind?"

"Don't be silly! You said we can travel on your vacations and on long weekends like this one. And do it in luxury, thanks to your new promotion.

"Look at this place," she said, waving around the inside of the RV. "Microwave, TV, a full-size shower. All the comforts of home."

"And don't forget that queen-size bed in the bedroom in back," he said, giving her a meaningful wink and his boyish grin.

"Why, David Miller! Are you propositioning me?"

He grinned again but, instead of answering, pointed to the oversized gift bag, overflowing with festive tissue that her friend Ellen had handed them just before they got in the RV. "This is from all of us at the Stitching Post," she'd told them. "A going away gift, but you can't open it until you're on your way..."

"Think we're far enough on our way to open that?"

"I don't see why not," Sylvia responded and lifted the big bag onto her lap. She reached into the bag and pulled out a heavy cylinder wrapped in yellow tissue. "The tag says to open this one first."

Dave glanced over as she peeled back the bright yellow paper.

"Oh yum, sparkling cider! The tag says it's to christen our RV on its maiden voyage. Think it's okay if we drink it instead of smashing it over the hood?

"I don't think they'll mind."

She reached in the bag again then laughed and held up a pair of champagne flutes. "I suspect you're right, honey."

"Smart ladies," he said, returning his attention to the road. "What else did they put in that bag? A picnic hamper? Maybe a CD by The Londoners or Barry Manilow?"

"I don't think so," she said. "It's something big...but it's soft." She pulled the bulky parcel from the bag and began to pull back the multi-colored layers of tissue covering it. As the last layer fell away, she gasped in surprise.

"What is it, honey?" Dave asked, taking his eyes from the road at the sound. "Are you okay?"

"Oh, Dave!" she sobbed. "They've finished my travel quilt. *Our* travel quilt." Tears flowed down her cheeks, but she smiled as she stroked the beautifully stitched cranberry hearts. "It's just like I always pictured it. Only bigger."

He reached into his pocket and pulled out his handkerchief then passed it to her. "It's beautiful...just like you," he said as she wiped her eyes. "This heart looks familiar. Isn't that the pattern on your jewelry box?"

"And on my necklace," she said, fingering the newly repaired pendant. "That's why I planned to use it to make a hanging quilt. I thought I'd embroider the names of the places we visited on the blocks." She unfolded the quilt slightly. "Everyone in the group must have all worked on this. See how big it is?"

"Big enough to fit that queen-sized bed?"

Sylvia unfolded more of the quilt and nodded. "I think so.

Oh my goodness, look at this, honey."

She pointed to a heart in the middle of the quilt where her friends had embroidered the date and the words "Bon Voyage, Sylvia and Dave!"

"Very nice," Dave agreed.

"I can't wait to embroider our first destination on here," Sylvia said, reaching for the quilting bag she'd placed on the floor behind her seat when they packed. She pulled out a small portable quilt hoop and a skein of floss.

"Which memory heart do you think I should embroider first?"

"It doesn't matter to me, honey," he said, laying his hand over her smaller one. "So long as we're making all the memories together."

About the Authors:

During her first career, **Patricia Kiyono** taught elementary music, computer classes, elementary classrooms, and junior high social studies. She now teaches music education at the university level.

She lives in southwest Michigan with her husband, not far from her children and grandchildren. Current interests, aside from writing, include sewing, crocheting, scrapbooking, and music. A love of travel and an interest in faraway people inspires her to create stories about different cultures.

Stephanie Michels considers herself a "Jill of All Trades" having worked as a computer trainer, advertising copywriter, cosmetologist, personnel agent, radio DJ, magazine columnist, and a financial planner among other things. She recently left the corporate world to focus on writing full time.

Raised in Michigan, she lived in South Carolina, Missouri, and Germany, before returning to the Mitten State to raise her family. When she isn't writing, you can usually find her reading, playing word games on the computer, or spending time with family and friends.

The Calico Heart is her first novel published with writing partner, Patricia Kiyono.

Astraea Press

Pure. Fiction.

www.astraeapress.com

Made in the USA
Charleston, SC
27 March 2013